My Dear Ellie

For Eleanor, Your Love is Eternal

Aisha Urooj

Dedicated to love and friendship

Prologue

Ever had a friend that made you smile on the darkest of days?

I do! I have my best friend Ellie.

If you are lucky enough to have a best friend, what would you do for them? Would you stand up for them, fight the last person on earth for them, die for them...give them your kidney?

Said yes so far? Surely your love for your friend is wonderful....but what if I ask: would you be willing to live through heartbreaks over a thousand lifetimes just to be with your friend together til the last breath?

Would you only do it for your best friend or someone else you love....It gets a little complicated now, doesn't it?

How will you choose, I wonder.

Chapter One: Distant Storms

I see lightning flash brilliantly outside. Just like the scene of any supernatural horror movie. The rain pelting noisily down my window cannot stop my reverie as I think about my best friend Ellie.

Eleanor James. Ellie, for short.

My partner-in-crime and life adventures as far as I can remember. My most vivid memory of a young Ellie running towards me with her golden hair braided into two. Her aura, a beacon and sunshine. I am a contrast of dark tresses, much like the present-day ominous storm clouds creeping outside.

I think back to the memory. I remember that as I looked at my own dark curls, open and unabandoned, I decided that I don't like Ellie's hair being tied up. I tug open her braids and her hair cascade open like two golden waterfalls. She looks stunned for a moment then she throws back her head and laughs like the beaming sun.

Eleanor James and Cassandra Grace. Ellie and Cassie.

Two girls that looked so apart yet like peas in a pod...like Spongebob and Patrick, her favourite mischievous best friend duo from the cartoon show.

"Oh Cassie, my pineapple", she would say with her favourite expression. "Why did you do that? Why did you open my braids?"

"I can't see the wind blow your hair around when it is tied up *like that,*" I reply impatiently. "Don't be a gold-i-*locked.*" My young self chimed, with an know-it-all air, as if that settled the matter. "I want you to be free Ellie."

It was only with Ellie could I do such a thing. Being around her made me bold, like she wasn't a different person, but simply an extension of me or the person I could be. When she dropped out of high school, I didn't think twice. I wanted to be wherever she was. Go wherever she went. She had her dreams of being a star. I had no clue what I wanted to do.

"Why do you want to be a star?", I ask her for the umpteenth time, thinking that maybe her answer would set off my own inspiration. Her eyes starts to sparkle, like she had been waiting to answer the same question she had answered me only numerous times before. "Because I can choose to be anyone I want," says Ellie. She does her best impression of royalty, waving her hand imperiously to an invisible audience and I imagine witnessing the public screaming and calling her name: "Eleanor, Eleanor, Eleanor". Her legions of adoring fans waiting tirelessly for her every word, searching for her in every street and copying her every gesture. Their new darling and Hollywood's latest obsession.

I never got jealous of the great things that was surely destined for her. For me, she was my Ellie. My anchor while I drifted through life. Drifted aimlessly to find a purpose, a reason, a calling. Floating away in the endless expanse while she held me and bound me to this earth like a lifeline. A warmth, a hug on a cold day. Ellie, my best friend.

She never did braid her hair again. She left her hair open in golden waves. She said that she did it for me and that whenever anyone wants to braid her hair, she says her best friend wants her to be a mermaid with beach waves for hair and not a rapunzel in her locked tower. I guess my reason made sense to her as a kid.

It is times like the present when I think of Ellie the most. As the storm outside grew louder, I want to call her and hear her voice. Where would she be right now? Probably somewhere outside warm and sunny. Most likely at a rehearsal or audition somewhere, lining up with countless other hopefuls to catch their next big break. We had never been separated by this much distance before. Apart in different cities, stretched across the globe. No, I won't break her focus with yet another call for support. Cassandra Grace, friend-in-distress. A clingy, hopeless, depressing shadow.

No, I am ok. I will wait. Wait for her next call, telling me excitedly about her latest acting gig. Her voice, alive and bright... bringing a smile to anyone caught in her whirlwind of energy. Her laugh trickling down your soul. This time I will only listen. Listen to her thoughts uninterrupted.

I had stopped going to her auditions with her. Not that I didn't want to. I didn't have her boundless energy and I had my menial job. A way to pay the bills. At first she went to the local theatres. Then she went to the aspiring actors hot spots in major cities. Further and further grew her circle, like a bird spreading her wingspan til I couldn't keep up with her pace or flight anymore. So I stayed.

She would call every so often and I looked forward to her visits. My small, dingy apartment seemed brighter and bigger with her presence. No matter how far she went, she came back the same girl. For her, my place became a place to stop and recharge. A refuge to be Ellie. Not almost famous Eleanor James. The actress who starred in so and so. A rising sensation.

Chapter Two: A Time of Firsts

My first memory of Ellie is not so clear. That week I had lost my granddad and I was swinging listlessly on the playground swings. Grandpa used to swing me on the swings and carry me on his shoulders. He secretly brought me candies. I missed playing with him.

I might have been alone in the playground that day, crying. She appeared suddenly and wiped away my tears with her little hands. I remember a golden little angel holding my hand and me not feeling so alone anymore. She was always like that. Through high school and numerous heartbreaks. Through countless failed attempts at love and in life. She was there to wipe the tears.

When she is not near, I imagine her voice giving me advice or comforting words.

Sometimes I wonder if her angelicness is a figment of my imagination. I quickly banish the thought. If it were so, then there will be no hope for humanity. She is just selfless and I am lucky to have her as my friend. She knows me well as she has suffered setbacks the same way I have. Only difference is that she emerged from the experience, untainted and light. Perhaps we balance each other out this way: I am the reason in life, while she is the rhyme.

It isn't always a perfect harmony in our friendship and it is not like we havent had our fair share of arguments or disagreements before. Always over something trivial. James Evans or Chris Gemsworth, which actor would we date? or deciding who would wear what outfit? or what takeout we should get? or what restaurant to visit and then argue about what table to sit at that restaurant? Harmless minor squabbles. There was a time our friendship was put to a test, Ellie got into a car accident and didn't tell me.

I don't hear her talk too much about it except sometimes when she says her back hurt and the painkillers not doing anything to ease it. It was the first time she had kept her feelings secret. She never kept secrets about something important. She said she didn't want to tell me about the accident as it would have frightened me. Later I find her experience was more harrowing than that. She came onto the path of a moving car while escaping an attempted assault by someone who was very intoxicated.

It came with the industry: the uncertainty. I heard whispers when we attended some acting events or afterparty together. Gossips overheard in the ladies room. I always remained uneasy when Ellie went alone. She assured me there was nothing to worry. I almost believed her if it weren't for this uneasy feeling I had. Maybe I felt overprotective? I was older than Ellie by more than a month. Or maybe it was because Ellie was so trusting, even with strangers.

No, I was being overprotective. Ellie was friendly sure but was also smart and perceptive about people, both the good and the bad. She figured out about John way before I had.

∞∞∞

John Damon was my first boyfriend. A charming, unassuming high school senior who got along with everyone. He didn't really fit in any clique nor did he attempt to. Maybe that is why I fell for him, or it might have been as simple as him complimenting my hair. He said that he had never seen curls like mine, "rolling around like ocean waves" is how he described them. Ellie said that I had blushed. I simply stuttered a thank you to John and nudged Ellie lightly to stop her cheeky grin from spreading even further.

Ellie had warned me beforehand about John's interest. and of course I hadn't believed her. She said she often caught him looking for me in the hallways, him smiling brightly at my sight, him waiting and hoping for a chance to talk to me. The whole John situation was, in her words, "Oh so romantic!". I sighed. At least I had been warned and somewhat prepared. I managed to stammer a response to his compliment this time otherwise normally I would have just blinked or become mute....or panicked, blushed and vanished to my hiding spot in the library. I am so pathetic.

Ellie had caught me doing it before but this time she was not having it. Not with John.

I am glad I didn't. He turned out as great as Ellie had predicted. Never pressured me to speak more than I could. I would feel a warm feeling wash over me when I thought of him, his good nature and his patience. He saw things in me that I couldn't see myself. I wasn't so sure that I deserved his praise when he said that "I had the soul of a poet" and that my solitude was "not rejection of the world but rather contemplation of it." He said that the world would sometimes feel too busy, loud, fast and chaotic for a shy girl and that I just needed "time and space to process it all."

He said that he felt that I had an "old soul". At the time I wouldn't have understood what the phrase really would mean to me.

Before meeting them both, I had wanted to fit in and have friends. God must have been listening to my silent prayers as both John and Ellie came into my life.

∞∞∞

My first date with John goes disastrously at the beginning as I lost my ability to speak words. This only happened to me when I got really anxious, so to my horror and grief I had instant case of selective mutism and could only answer him back with not words, but by either nodding yes or no.

"Cassie is there any restaurant you would like to go to?"

I shake my head silently.

"We could go for movies. Which movie would you like to see?"

Thinking of being alone in the dark with John makes me nervous and I respond with a deer in the headlights expression.

John sensing my nervousness changes the question, "Perhaps we could just go for a walk?"

I am relieved at this choice and nod in agreement.

As we walk around our small town, I realize that John is looking at the familiar paths and houses with the eyes of a stranger. I become more curious about him and ask him how long he had been living here.

"I haven't been here long, I moved here maybe two years ago but coincidentally you were one of the first people I met!" I am surprised as I don't remember meeting him. He continues, "It was my first day in town and things hadn't been going great. Everything here felt new and strange. I was riding my bike hoping to come across some kids my age when I bumped into you. You were busy reading a Harry Potter book. I have read that book series too! I wanted to talk to you about the book and to apologize for bumping into you but you just quietly said 'sorry' and quickly disappeared. I tried looking for you everywhere that day, but I couldn't find you. I hadn't seen anyone move so fast before!"

I blush at his story, thinking about all the trouble he went through in trying to find me but I am pleased to know that he likes Harry Potter too. We spend more time talking about the novels and I find myself talking more to him than I had to anyone else before, besides Ellie.

Chapter Three: Sugar Sweet

Fall is my favorite time of the year, not only is the weather the perfect blend of not too cold or warm, the beautiful colorful panorama of reds, greens, yellows and oranges foliage on the trees but also because of Halloween, the only occasion where we can freely ask for and receive sweets to our hearts' content.

According to my dentist, he had never seen someone with such a bad case of sweet tooth like mine but Ellie would make me feel better by saying that it was because I was naturally 'sugar sweet'. By the time we turn thirteen, Ellie wants to retire our annual tradition of trick-or-treating.

Every year, as long as I have known Ellie, we went together gathering candies in our co-ordinated halloween costumes. My parents tell me that before meeting Ellie, I had been too shy to do it alone or even to do it with them by my side.

"What should we dress as this year?"

"Should we be mermaids? We can do sparkly makeup with glitters and everything, and put seashells on our hair?", suggests Ellie.

"Hmmm..glitter might be messy and we will have trouble walking with our tails. If we slow down walking, we won't get to the houses fast enough and they will run out of the best candies!"

"You have a point...and we already went as Disney princesses last year remember. You wanted to be Belle and I went as Aurora. We should do something completely different for our last year trick-or-treating."

"Why are we not doing it again next year?", I ask sadly, thinking about not getting any candies next year.

"Because we are thirteen. 13...we should stop in the halloween spirit and the lucky number! Besides, too many people ask about our age and we don't look as cute as the little kids. We should leave the tradition to them and move on to more grownup things."

"Remember when people thought we were so adorable dressed up in our fruits costumes? We had the biggest stash that year! It took weeks to finish all the candies!", I reminisce fondly.

"Yeah...I don't how we thought of dressing as our favorites fruits, you as a prickly pineapple and me as a plump strawberry, and it felt a little silly wearing those huge costumes but everyone loved it."

"What should we do this year? I can't think of anything..."

"I got it! We should dress as something we want to be when we grow up.... I can dress up like a movie star!"

"But Ellie...I don't know what I want to be when I grow up. What will I do?"

"We can pick a career from a hat? I can put random ones into a hat and you can pick one up and dress up as that?"

"Sounds good, I can't think of anything else so let's do it!"

Ellie would write a bunch of random careers on little pieces of paper and then place it in a bag for me to choose from. I pick one piece of paper to read what my costume would be and it said "Movie writer" in Ellie's handwriting. I had to get creative with my tricky costume and I dressed as what I thought a writer would look like, dressed in all black, with a french beret, black sunglasses and mock turtleneck sweater, carrying a long paper scroll with an enormous feather pen in hand, waiting to write down furiously when inspiration struck...even in the middle of conversations. I should have added a cup of coffee for effect, even if I hadn't started drinking coffee yet. That year, for our last Halloween as kids, we would end our much beloved annual tradition of trick-or-treating dressed up like our dream future grown-up versions, Ellie as the movie star and me as a movie writer.

This year, my favourite season fall once again turned out memorable in another way. I was delighted when I found out that John shares my love for the season too. He thinks that fall is the best season for playing outdoors and says that he liked piling on the leaves and jumping into them as a kid. Now, during fall, he likes walking and hiking especially with the picturesque backdrop of our small town. This year, the town looks and feels even more beautiful than it ever did before maybe because this time I had John with me. We had already been on a few dates by now and he and I would soon share our first kiss. My first at age sixteen and a half.

We were walking towards the park after we had bought some icecream. He was quieter than usual. Usually he would fill in my shy silences with pleasant conversation. We reached a small bridge in the park but he stopped walking. I look up at him to see why and I see him deep in thought. His eyes linger on mine, brown eyes shining like amber. I must have blushed for he gently reached out for my hand. My small olive hands contrasting against his pale long fingers. He would often compare our fingers to each other, put our palms together and remark at how small my fingers were to his. I can feel the warmth of his hands and I feel myself blush again. He held my hand and lifted it to his lips and gives the gentlest of kiss, as if he was afraid I might be startled by any sudden movement. He then looks at me and slowly reaches down to kiss. I close my eyes and feel his lips close over mine.

He tastes sweet like the chocolate icecream he had. I wonder if I tasted sweet to him? When I open my eyes, I see him looking slightly dazed. I have an urge to giggle but I don't. I feel oddly emboldened by his awestruck expression and I reach out my hand to trace the scar on his face with my fingertips. The one that I know he felt self-conscious about and the one I had wanted to touch for the longest time. I see him blush slightly more and I am completely smitten by him.

We walk to our homes, hand in hand after our sweet exchange. Ellie is over the moon when I tell her...and also slightly jealous. I am amused by her revelation that she is jealous of my first kiss. She reminded me shortly that hers was with a "icky nine year old neighbour at a cousin's birthday party during a game of truth or dare when she was eight." She says that I am so lucky that I got to share my first kiss with someone I wanted.

I suppose it is lucky to share the first kiss with someone you really like, no matter at what age you do.

Chapter Four: Soup Kitchen

E llie and I are not exactly what you will call 'studious', but we try our best and do put serious effort into our school assignments and homeworks.

For our creative writing assignment, we are given the topic of 'Plight of the Homeless' to write on and we decide to help each other with the four-page essay. As we sat together in the public library, brainstorming for hours, we only manage to come up with a few ideas to write on. As we looked at each other's progress, we realized that we needed a different approach as we had only filled two-thirds of a page between the two of us, almost half a page for me and a few lines for Ellie. Our slow pace was becoming a problem as the deadline for the assignment was fast approaching.

"Argghh...why is this so hard to write about?", I say frustrated.

"Yeah...it is hard", says Ellie, scratching her head.

"I don't know...I guess we should consider ourselves privileged if we can't even write about what it feels like to be poor!"

"Cassie....you just gave me an idea! Maybe we need to see first hand and experience it ourselves?"

"Ellie, I don't know if my parents would let me become homeless, even if it is just for a short while and for good grades."

"Not become homeless, silly! I meant we should do what great actors and writers do for a role and go to the place where they can see real people for themselves. We should volunteer at a homeless shelter!"

"Good idea! We could do that....but we should do it quickly though, the assignment is due soon."

That weekend, Ellie would sign us both up to volunteer at a soup kitchen and we arrive at the location early in the morning.

"Hi! Are you Ms. Carla Smith? I am Eleanor James and this is my friend Cassandra Grace. We both signed up to volunteer this weekend."

"Yes, I am Carla Smith. Thank you for showing up on time. You are assigned to the kitchen today, you can go find the chef in the kitchen. He will let you know what you have to do."

Ms. Carla is a petite woman, dressed formally, with an serious expression on her face and cuts an authoritative figure. Her tone suggests that she is angry about something, I look at Ellie and she just shrugs her shoulder. We both go to the kitchen to look for the chef and find him to be in a better mood than the soup kitchen manager.

"Oh my, I have two little fairies helping me out in the kitchen today!", says the chef, who looked like he belonged in the North Pole and could pass for Santa Claus.

"Are you Santa?", asks Ellie and I smack my head at Ellie's predisposition of saying out loud what she thought.

The chef laughs, "People often call me Santa, but you can call me Mr. Chris as well!"

"Ok, thank you Mr. Chris! What would you like us to do?"

Mr. Chris assigns us to mopping and dusting duties at first and laughs heartily when Ellie asks for the Roomba. We quickly learn how to use the feather duster and mop and sweep up the place with an eager fervor.

Next, we are assigned with prepping the vegetables and Mr. Chris had to save me from myself, as I nearly enthusiastically chop my fingers off with my knife while cutting the carrots wildly. Ellie had thought that my tears were tears of joy and gratitude at being saved from grievous injury but I had already been crying because of the onions.

After we are done with the vegetables, Mr. Chris assigns us to the sink to wash the dishes. Between the two of us, we breeze through cleaning the dishes and making them shine. Mr. Chris now has run out of tasks for us to do.

"You girls have done everything and are still asking for more work?", laughs Mr. Chris. "Now only the cooking is left in the kitchen, which you can leave it up to me. Tell you what, go find Carla...I am sure she can use the two extra pairs of hardworking hands."

As we go searching for Ms. Carla, I secretly hope that we find the soup kitchen manager in a better mood by now. We find her and she crossly and abruptly assigns us with distributing food to the incoming soup kitchen patrons. There are all types of people coming in need of food, some are young, some are old, some are with little children. It is eye-opening experience for both Ellie and me and we stand quietly handing out slices of bread to each plate as they are brought forward. A frail looking man brings forward his plate and asks me for my name and I am too startled to say anything back. I can see his clothes are torn in places and dishevelled. His hands are also trembling but he has friendly and kind looking eyes. I quickly hand him out four slices of bread instead of the two that we are instructed to do. I see Ms. Carla come stand next to me and I am worried that I would be told off for my action.

"It helps if you see them as people", she says shortly. "It wouldn't hurt if you could talk with them a little too."

She leaves after saying this and I am left feeling red-faced and ashamed.

"That is not fair!", says Ellie. "You get shy around new people Cassie...that doesn't mean that you are being a snob or something like that. She doesn't even know you well!"

"You are right Ellie but Ms. Carla is normally like this...don't feel bad about what she said Cassie", says a familiar voice. I look up to see that it is John, smiling kindly at me. "I think that she is more mad at herself than anyone else amd wishes that she could do more for the people coming here....though I don't agree with the way she does it, I myself prefer Mr. Chris' attitude..but she herself has been volunteering here since she was a teenager and been working here longer than anyone else. The people coming here are always grateful for the help."

"I didn't know that you volunteered here John?", I ask surprised.

"Did you come here for an assignment too?", asks Ellie.

"Assignment? I come here to volunteer sometimes as I like talking to the people...there are some veterans who come here too and I like hearing about their life stories."

After we are done helping with distributing the food, John takes us both to meet some of the people. We spend the remainder of the evening listening to the people who share with us snippets about their lives. Some of them are suffering from mental illnesses, others are having a tough life after a failed business and some are battling substance addictions. One thing is for sure that for the people coming to the soup kitchen, life is a daily battle for survival. At the end of the day, Mr. Chris joins us from the kitchen and gives us volunteers a plate of sandwiches to share. Ellie and I both thank John and Mr. Chris for showing us how to give something back to the community and to them for making a positive difference to the people around them.

We volunteer for another day at the soup kitchen and after that we would often return to do so at least a couple of times in the year.

As for the assignment, we both receive good grades for our essay submission. My essay titled 'It helps if you see them as people" was well-liked by our teacher and she said that I captured the snapshot of peoples' life with clarity and empathy.

Ellie was profoundly impacted by our volunteer experience and years later, as a famous movie star, she would donate a portion of her paycheck to the same soup kitchen that we had volunteered at. Ellie said that upon receiving the check, Ms. Carla, the seemingly stern soup kitchen manager, had been moved to tears and had given her a hug. I guess John had been right about her.

Chapter Five: Winter Wonderland

Winter is Ellie's favorite time of the year. If she had been mother nature, she would have turned all her lands into a winter wonderland, the trees would have had ornaments of ice sparkling like gems in the sunlight and the streets would have been blankets of soft, fluffy snow all year long. She even loves the warmth and cheer of the crowds during the holiday season and would often drag me to our town's mall. I would rather do anything else in the whole world than to be at the mall during the holiday season or before a snowstorm.

I hate the bleakness of the cold weather and I would rather avoid places where there are tons of people. Call me Ebeneezer, Scrooge or Grinch, but I don't like exchanging gifts on Christmas and would rather spend the time with my loved ones than go look desperately for a gift with other equally desperate gift searchers in the mall. I guess I just don't have the patience for it.

It is the day after Christmas and Ellie wants us to go to the mall to look at the sales.

"Didn't we just receive gifts on Christmas? Why do we need to go to the mall to get more stuff?"

"Cassie...you are missing the point, it will be fun. Everyone will be there!"

"Exactly! Everyone will be there. How would that be fun?"

"It is so nice to see people being happy at this time of year. We can talk to them about how their holidays went. Exchange stories about the food and gifts."

"Can't we do that at school? *after* the holidays, when they will have even more stuff to tell..."

"You really don't want to go, do you?", says Ellie laughing. "Still it is not as bad as last year when you faked a flu."

"It was a flu! I was really sick!"

"Cassie, you sneezed like once and had no fever. Ok, if you don't want to go to the mall, can we at least go to the park. I want to see the snow! We actually had a good snowfall this year."

Thinking that the park would be without the crowds, who will all be flocking to the malls today, I agree to go with Ellie out in the cold weather. The park is nice and quiet and we really did get a lot of snow this year. We kept walking in silence in the ankle deep snow, with only our footsteps echoing in eerie quietness. We walk til we reach the section of the park that borders to the ravine, I start to turn back but Ellie insists to keep going.

"Just a little more further Cassie, I want to see the trees in the ravine...they will all have snow on them."

"Ok Ellie."

We walk to the edge of the ravine and see a wintery landscape open before our eyes. The sun shines at the exact moment to reveal a vast white landscape with snow-laden trees, the snow reflecting the sun at some points and glittering like an white ocean. At that moment I realize the quiet but breathtaking beauty of winter. So this is how Ellie saw it, I think to myself.

We stay there admiring for a while longer then start to head back towards the park but Ellie wants me to see one more thing before we leave, hidden in an open space between the tall trees is a spot where the sun is shining and rising above on the ground is an angel made of snow. The snow angel figure looks so mysterious in its surrounding that I look at Ellie in amazement.

"Look Ellie, there is a angel here! How did this get here?"

I look at the statue and it looks divine in the snowy backdrop, two hands clasped to each other as in prayer and wings spread open wide behind the shoulders. The details in the angel make it seem almost lifelike, with the delicate feathers etched in the snowy wings and the details in the angelic face. I look closer into the statue and see two green eyes looking back at me.

"It looks so life-like Ellie, the angel even has green stones for eyes...I would have thought angels would have blue or violet eyes, isn't that how they are in paintings? The eye colour is so unusual but the statue really looks lovely here. What a nice thing to do by whoever that made it...", I add.

"So you like it? It's for you, it is your christmas present Cassie. Surprise! I know you didn't want a present this year, even though you gave presents yourself but it wouldn't had been fair not to give you something in return."

"It is beautiful Ellie! I love it...but how did you make this? I didn't know that you could sculpt with snow.."

"It wasn't me, I just helped keep the surprise and keep you distracted from someone."

"Me distracted? From who?"

"Merry Christmas Cassie! Did you like the surprise?"

I turn to see that it was John who was the mysterious sculptor.

"John! It was you...I never could have imagined it."

"So what do you think about the angel? I made the eyes the same color as yours Cassie."

I blush deeply and barely manage to thank both John and Ellie for their gift. "Both of you kept this a secret for me? What a wonderful present. Thank you..."

I am deeply touched by their gesture and as I thank them, I become emotional and start to cry. Both Ellie and John collectively groan at the sight of my tears.

"Oh Good Lord, she started her tearworks! She *must* have liked the surprise..", says John laughing.

"Careful Cassie, you tears might flood the snow angel and melt it away!", adds Ellie.

"Very funny you too! Let me cry... I am so lucky to have you both in my life!" Both Ellie and John beam at my words and smile as I give them a hug.

"Merry Christmas Cassie!"

After taking some pictures together with the snow angel, we walk back home together. We left the snow angel as she was by the ravine, bathing in sunlight. There she continues to look at passerbys with her green eyes, waiting to surprise anyone else who went there to admire the wintry landscape, the frost-covered branches, to enjoy the beauty of the season.

Chapter Six: Vive L'Amour

Valentine's day was fast approaching. Ellie would always make a big deal out of Valentines. I have to admit, I was fond of the pink hearts, teddy bears, chocolate filled, red roses infused love bomb confetti of a holiday as well. It was hard for me to feel surly that day, whether I was single or not. The worst I would feel was wistful, looking at the loving couples and wondering when it would be my time for love. The best I would feel would be like this valentine with John.

Ellie's efforts on Valentine's would always become, as she said: "extra resourceful and full of spirit and cheer." She plays secret valentine on February 14th. She thinks I don't know about it but I figured it out. Each year, all the girls in our class would receive a single rose in their lockers from a "secret admirer." I know that Ellie does it to spread around the love, to make the girls feel the magic of the day and not feel lonely, to look for-ward to that rose no matter how their valentine's was going.

Usually both Ellie and I would walk to school together but on that day, she would make some excuse. A flu, a missed alarm, a missing shoe or a last minute early morning class meeting that I wasn't invited to despite being in the same class. Each excuse more elaborate than the other.

With any scheme or diversion that she could come up with, she would arrive earlier than me in order to play cupid. Despite her early start to the day, there would be something amiss if she did not dress in all pink or red, from her clothes, her accessories to her shoes. She really was spirited about Valentines.

Ellie wondered for weeks what John had planned for me. I on the other hand, despite having a loving boyfriend like John, hadn't thought about it. I was too busy thinking about the excuse Ellie would make this time to miss our walk together to school. But John wasn't distracted by Ellie's annual odd and secretive behaviour around Valentine's as I was and he would get me something.

He finds me alone in the hallway before class. He shyly hands me a small box and I look at it with curiousity. My emotions get the better of me and I panic and say that I didn't remember to get him anything. He laughs at the thought and presses me to open his gift. I open the box to find a pair of small earrings twinkling with two little red glass hearts. They are beautiful. How could he be so romantic? I wondered how I would thank him.

"Do you like them?"

"Yes I do, I like them very much. They are so pretty!"

"I am glad you liked them Cassie."

"Thank you John...", I say, trying to find the words that would describe how much he meant to me. "I...I...am glad that I didn't run away from you..", I end lamely.

"I am *very* glad about that too", jokes John.

"What I meant to say is that I haven't felt this safe to be myself around anyone before. I feel extremely lucky to be with you."

"Cassie....I feel the same way." He pauses. It looks like he wants to say something more... but he doesn't.

"I really.....like the gift. Thank you so much", I say, chickening out, when I really wanted was to tell him how I felt about him.

I still felt like a toad for not getting him something for Valentine's too but I put aside my guilt to tiptoe up and kiss him softly on his cheek, seeing him blush and smile made me feel slightly better. I start to head for class but John isn't ready to let go of me yet. He pulls me in, bringing me closer to him for a kiss and I gasp in surprise. He then kisses me even harder, holding me tight like he had never held me before and I melt into his embrace. His kiss clearly tells me what he had wanted to say before.

Although the three little words remain unsaid between us, it seemed like at that moment it was on both our minds.

I walk into class feeling like I was floating on air.

Ellie sighed happily when she heard about this. She lives for these moments. One of the reasons why she wants to be an actress is to play romantic roles in movies. And to kiss the hottest superstar...that is her life goal too.

Years after high school, Ellie would continue the tradition of celebrating Valentines together. She would hold an all girl's day, usually close to valentines and each year she would end the day with a toast: "May we live for love and may Love live among us. Mortality weeps for her frailness, Love marvels us with her strength. Love laughs eternal! Vive l'amour ma chérie, Cheers!"

Chapter Seven: Smile in the Face of Sweet Sorrow

My romance with John didn't last long in high school, life can sometimes be cruel that way.

John's dad worked for a division of the United Nations, which shuttled his family all over the world. They lived in Cambodia, Cyprus, Tunisia, Japan, France, Switzerland; it worked out as such that around every two years it was a different country. John had spend most of his life moving from one place to another. His dad had another reposting somewhere remote and now he had to go from here too.

I cried when John moved, I didn't care to know where he was going, just that he was leaving. He tried his best to console me but I was inconsolable. I wish now I hadn't been so self absorbed. I wish now that I had been stronger and showed empathy for his situation. It couldn't have been easy moving from one place to another, leaving your friends behind and starting anew at another school, each time not knowing how long you would be there. Even though we hadn't said the words to each other, I knew how much he loved me and that leaving me was really hard for him too but being seventeen, he couldn't just leave his family.

Fear made me terribly insecure and my thoughts became grim. How would we be together anymore? How would a seventeen year old boy remember me? I thought that he would surely forget me. He would find another girl with hair rolling like ocean waves.

I felt broken. At sixteen, I didn't or couldn't grasp the concept of a long distance relationship. I didn't want to stay in touch with him that way. Every phone call, every text and every picture made me miss him more. I stopped answering him back. He wasn't near me anymore and my fears would have had me lose him forever.

Fate had something else in store for our young love. After many years, John would finally find me. Til that day came, however, I was fated to listless dates with matches that either felt unromantic in nature or worse, platonic. I didn't know then he would come back into my life. I didn't know then that he never forgot me.

Our ill-fated separation at the time had left me hollow and in tears for a long while. It made Ellie miserable seeing me like this too.

"Cassie! Can you please smile? I can't bear to see you this sad!"

Looking at her concerned face, I try to smile but it was harder to do than I thought.

"What was that?", asks Ellie.

"What was what?"

"*That?*", She says, pointing to my face.

"I was trying to smile."

"Oh!", she says, then after a short pause, "It looked like you were trying to grimace." She says it seriously. "Or that you are constipated."

That makes me giggle, which sets off Ellie giggling too. We stop giggling after a while.

"Um...Cassie? Remember that day when I thought I had lost Hammy?"

"Hammy? Your pet hamster?", I ask slightly puzzled at her train of thought.

"Yes?"

"Yeah I remember that cute fuzzball. You thought he got accidentally flushed in the bathroom but he just had been hiding in your fuzzy slippers."

"Yes! I had cried so much thinking he was gone and that I couldn't even plan for his funeral", she says remembering sadly. After some thought she asks,"Why do you think he was hiding?"

"Hmm....maybe he didn't like to wear those bowties you made him wear?"

"What? No that *can't* be the reason! He looked so dashing!... and I wanted to make him look handsome for the lady hamsters!", says Ellie quickly. Next she adds thoughtfully, "But when he went missing, I thought I had lost him forever but he just had been hiding in plain sight and he came back. Maybe John will be back too, you just need to have faith in him. Don't lose hope Cassie."

I am struck by the fact that Ellie compares my heartbreak with John to Hammy. I think back to the frightened little hamster with a bowtie. Ellie's words "dashing" "handsome hamster" echo in my brain and despite my best efforts not to, it makes me smile.

Seeing my dark mood lifted, Ellie looks delighted. "I missed your smile! Oh my dear Cassie, as long as you can think of one happy thought and smile, everything will be ok."

Her thought and her concern for me touches my heart and lessens the pain of my first heartbreak, I don't feel alone in my sadness. I don't want to make her any more miserable for me than she already was so I listen to her advice, but it was very hard for my teenager self, when emotions felt especially magnified, to continue back to normalcy and to keep going to the high school where everything reminded me of him.

I didn't have to stay long after John moved, however, as Ellie had decided to pursue her acting dreams away from high school.

I could barely survive high school with Ellie by my side. John had gone. How in the world could I do it without her? It was an easy decision for me to make and without any hesitation, I support Ellie's idea and plan to drop out of high school along with her. We just had to think of a way to survive telling about our decision to our parents together.

Chapter Eight: A Parent's Heart

O ur two sets of parents freaked. Two young girls suddenly dropping out of academia, barely just turned seventeen and not even finishing high school? Unheard of! I was accused of being a lemming to Ellie, willing to follow her blindly to the sea. Ellie was accused of living in a fantasy world. Ellie, being Ellie, was finally able to convince our parents to give us a chance.

She must have inherited her gift to negotiate from her lawyer parents. We had a deal that if we weren't successful within a couple of years (two or three at most), we could go back to finishing our high school diplomas and then go for our university degrees. I could see the decision tearing our parents apart but either it was agreeing to Ellie's proposal or losing us both. They knew how stubborn Ellie could be. They knew I wouldn't leave her for the world. Both Ellie and I talk on the phone to discuss whether or not we had convinced our parents.

"What do you think? Do you think that they will agree?"

"I am pretty sure my parents are going to say yes", says Ellie. "I always win and usually they give in by the seventeenth time I ask them."

"I don't know about my parents...they were pretty worried especially mom. I think it really shocked her."

"You can't back out now Cassie. We need to stay strong...think of the freedom! No more boring classes...we can be on our own exploring the world together!"

"Ellie... I am still thinking about what my mom said. She said that when I was born, it was like her heart started beating outside her chest, outside as me. She doesn't want me to stop being her baby. She can't believe that I want to drop out of school and move out."

"Cassie...it is going to happen sooner or later. You are your own person too and need to understand the world around you and stand up on your own two feet. Sooner or later you will have to stop holding on to your parents' hands and become independent. Deep down, they would want you to follow your heart and happiness. Besides, we have made them a iron-clad promise that we will try out for our dreams and if we weren't successful, we will go back to doing what they want...go to high school and then university."

"Ellie, I am not like you. You are so sure what you want to do in your life, you have always been sure of it...I don't even know what I want to do..."

"Stay with me Cassie and we will figure it out together, like we always do!"

"You know Ellie what my parents said...they said that it gets harder to go back to high school once you leave it in the middle."

"Hmmm...that might be true but it is not like we would go back to the same high school. We could take online courses for the courses that are missing to get our diploma as well."

Ellie was right, I hadn't thought about that option. It makes me feel better.

"So you don't think that it will be hard to go back to studies?"

"No, it won't...it's because we made a promise to our parents. That reason would make it easier to go back."

"So do you think that they will agree Ellie?"

"Yes, absolutely! I am sure they will."

Surprisingly, our parents did agree just as Ellie had predicted. Now that I think about it, both Ellie and I were tremendously fortunate in having parents that were so supportive and who gave us enough freedom to pursue our dream and forge our own paths in life. It must have been a hard decision for them to make but reluctantly and after much deliberation, they agreed.

Victorious, Ellie and I decidedly set off to pursue her acting career. As for myself, I was to figure out my own purpose in life out there in the real world.

Chapter Nine: Starry-Eyed

Ellie was often the star in our small high school plays. Lovely as Juliet, tragic as Ophelia, elegant as Guinevere. Nearly all the guys in school had a crush on her and all the girls wanted to be her. Her performance would get standing ovations but being the perfectionist that she is she was never satisfied. She wanted more.

She never wanted to go the traditional route of acting: High school drama classes, theatre, then acting roles. No, this was not Ellie. She wanted to star in original works now, at this very moment. Patience was never her forte. She believed in experience and a life fully lived as being the teacher.

She tried for her first auditions while still in high school. She said that homework and tests would interfere with her audition schedule. She was not fully free to attend all the auditions that she wanted. She had some success when she landed a small part in an soft drinks ad. She wanted to be more than just the pretty girl with the soda.

After dropping out of high school, we wanted to move out. Ellie and I decide to go the grownup route and look for our own apartment together, our parents want to help us but Ellie wants to do it on our own.

We finally reach a compromise, between parents and teenagers, for our living arrangement and Ellie' parents help us move into an apartment that they owned on the condition that we would contribute to the rent when we found jobs. Later, as Ellie's stardom grew and I also got more independent, we would move out in our own apartments but for the next few years, we were room mates and besties under one roof.

Initially, Ellie got small roles in movies. At least she was earning something, while I struggled to find a job. Luckily, my parents help with the job search and I get a part-time position as a secretary in an accounting firm of my dad's friend. The work was like watching paint dry but at least I had some money in my pocket.

While working there, during the long down times after tax season, it was increasingly hard for me to keep my eyes open out of the sheer boredom. So to pass the time I would pick up and read the books on finance that were lying around. Luckily, I managed to learn a few things about finance that would fuel my future part-time hobby and interest and even my lifestyle.

Determined, Ellie continues her hustle and works hard to get parts in movies, some of them even garnering some success. Ellie kept looking for a break-out role as so far the movies she was in were not up to par with her expectations. When I saw Ellie's first movie in a small theatre, I had mixed feelings.

"So how was I? How was the movie? What did you think?", Ellie had asked all in one breath.

Ellie's performance was amazing to be sure but something was missing. She could have shown so much more depth but the movie's script didn't take her there. She had it in her to be a surreal and sublime work of art, beyond what mere words and expressions could describe. It was like seeing a Da Vinci masterpiece but etched onto sand, having a transient and sadly, brief existence. You only get a brief glimpse of the masterwork before it is washed away by the incoming ocean tide. Her role had brief glimpses of her brilliance but she still needed the right canvas.

Ellie hadn't found that role yet or was it that the script meant for her hadn't been written? Her movie didn't generate much revenue but she got rave reviews for her part, more and more directors were becoming aware of her young talent and word of mouth was spreading fast.

Chapter Ten: Survival Basics

L ife in the real world kinda sucks. Life is struggle..let no one else tell you otherwise. I slowly realize the privileges of home that I had taken for granted.

I miss not having to do my own laundry, get my own food, then cook my own food, dust and clean the house and thousands of other chores that I did do while at home, but not all of them together as when living life like an independent adult. I wish there was a Survival basics 101 class taught in high school.

At least we don't have to worry about living arrangements like real adults (thank goodness!) and I really have the best room mate in the world as Ellie. She is open to whatever idea I suggest, the latest being trying to live life like a minimalist. The only problem is that we are both hopeless at it.

"I really like how we are not wasting our money getting things that we don't need Ellie. Living with less makes life so much stress-free and simple."

"You said it Cassie. We are helping the environment and reducing our global carbon footprint as well. Must do it to save the planet!"

"Yeah, only shopping at thriftstores for clothes is not bad at all. I don't even miss the online massive sales."

"Or the shoe sale that is going on."

"I didn't even know about that."

This is usually how the conversation started, with good intentions, but by the end, both of us will be looking at the websites with the aforementioned sales and then secretly ordering something as well. Both of us would then hide shopping bags in our closets after our online orders arrived. Sigh. At least we were trying.

As a Superstar, Ellie later becomes better at minimizing when she has to travel the world with only two suitcases and gets designers to dress her for free. By then, designers would compete aggressively for Ellie and she made sure to choose sustainable and eco-friendly fashion.

The seeds for the minimalist lifestyle was already sown long before, when we were teenagers trying to be responsible adults.

Chapter Eleven: Fortune Favors the Bold

Ellie didn't pay much attention to looks or concede to the pressures of her industry regarding physical appearances. She wasn't concerned, not that she ever needed to be, as she could make Venus blush in envy at her God-given divine countenance. She accepted the concepts of beauty and youth as being of a fleeting nature, infact, she embraced the idea with open arms. All that mattered to her was perfecting her acting talents irrespective of looks.

I, on the other hand, was not as wise nor as naturally gifted as Ellie was and did not share the same enthusiasm for my impending and inevitable progression to old age.

While brushing my hair one morning, I freaked out when I discovered that I had a grey one. I was near tears at the sight of my grey hair and what I thought was my body's cruel and untimely betrayal to my youth but somehow Ellie found it amusing.

"Ellie, can't you see I am distressed? How could you giggle at a time like this....when your friend is in *crisis*?," I say, dramatically.

She still finds it funny and continues to giggle.

"Elllie, why are you giggling? Stop it, It is not funny!"

"Oh Cassie, can't you see? You will grow old....then I will grow old. We will both grow old and wrinkly together," She says laughing. "We will have so much fun! We will become the two crackling old grannies, terrifying our adult children and plotting away and meddling in the lives of our young grandkids."

I am horrified by the thought of going completely grey. And old. And *wrinkly.*

I want to be angry at Ellie but I find that her delirium is contagious. Dangerously contagious. I see her unrestrained mirth and laughter and her twinkling blue eyes, forgetting my own neuroses for a little while, I start to laugh with her too.

Dinner that night was the same as the two nights before. It was the one item that I could make without burning: sandwiches. You see that my culinary expertise is limited to Peanut Butter & Jelly sandwiches expertly served and presented, in the optional shapes of either triangles, rectangles or squares. Looking at our familiar dinner option, Ellie wants to order takeout.

"Should we order Chinese or Indian?", I ask.

"Neither, we should go for Sushi. What do you think?"

"Sure we could...you know that Sushi is my middle name!"

"Really? I thought that it was PB&J", jokes Ellie

"Ha ha, very funny Eleanor."

"We should order calamari too!"

I think about our budget and do a quick calculation in my head. "But Ellie, that would be expensive..."

"Fine, let us only get calamari then!"

I pause to think. In the battle between being practical, staying on budgets and weekly quotas and the battle cry of our stomachs, hunger emerges the clear winner. I hear my stomach growling impatiently.

I quickly make a note in my mental to-do list to allocate a bigger room in our budget for emergency takeout situations and in the future, to devise a better plan that stays on budget when hungry. I reach for the phone to order our food.

Somehow we ended up ordering from all three takeouts, our dinner table a visual and olfactory cacophony of Indian, Chinese and Japanese cuisines. After consuming an outrageous amount of food, that even I am embarassed to think about, I reach for the fortune cookie from the takeout box to read my fortune. I am horrified at the words on the paper.

"Fortune favors the old?!," I wail. "I knew it...that grey hair from this morning was an omen! I am an antique", I say miserably.

"Fortune favors the *old*? That doesn't sound right, let me see that paper", says Ellie reaching for my fortune slip.

"Of course it is not right! I don't want to be favored only when I get old", I continue lamenting.

"Cassie, there is a crease right there...see? It says bold. Fortune favors the *bold*", Ellie corrects me.

"Really?.....What do you think that means?", I ask Ellie.

"Hmm maybe it means that you should try a different flavor jelly for your PB&J sandwich? You know, boldly switch it up and go where you have never gone before, on a dangerous culinary adventure with a new sandwich combination?"

"You are funny", I say sardonically, but by now fully recovered from my fortune cookie meltdown.

"What does your say?"

"It says that 'anxiety won't help your future or solve your problems. Only true happiness sets us free'."

"What do you think that means?"

"I am not sure...it is a mystery... it is talking about the future but I don't really have any anxieties", says Ellie reflecting on the fortune. She adds, "What I do know is that a full stomach makes me very happy so maybe the fortune cookie has a point!"

Both Ellie and I bask in the afterglow of our mighty feast and at our good fortune in having each other as friends to grow old with.

The fortune cookie was right in that being anxious about the future or anything else does not help solve problems or change the outcome, looking forward to adventures however does make life a whole lot more interesting.

Following our conversation, I do decide to go on a culinary adventure of-sorts and got myself a slow-cooker (remembering to include it in our budget) and start watching some cooking videos on the internet for inspiration, but mostly-truth be told- for much needed guidance on how to cook without burning the kitchen down.

After some interesting initial attempts, I am happy to say that I got fluent in making many edible and even delicious meals, our dinner would never again be peanut butter and jelly sandwiches.

Although, occasionally I would still make myself some late night when the mood struck, without Ellie knowing, for as the wisest would say, "Simplicity is the Key to Happiness."

True happiness really can be as simple as a homemade sandwich.

Chapter Twelve: Tattoo Mischief

E llie really wants to get a tattoo that she says would formally symbolize our foray into independence and adulthood. I am not going to take her side on this as I am oppose to any needles poking into any skin and shiver at just the thought. I don't even want to get the annual flu shot, because of my fear of needles and it is only that my fear of catching deadly influenza is greater that I manage to sit through the ordeal. I try to talk some sense into Ellie and deter her from getting permanently inked.

"Ellie...once you get a tattoo it is for life! Think about it...you don't even like last week's dress anymore. How would you stay with the same tattoo for years?"

"Cassie you can get a tattoo removed too...besides, tats are just so cool! It will make me look edgy!"

"Tattoo removal is painful and expensive!...and how would you choose a design that you will be happy with? Most people say to think about a design you want and after a year, if you still want it, only then should you go through with it..."

My words makes her pause a bit. "Fine Cassie, if you say so...I promise that I will give it serious thought and after deciding on a design, to wait first, really think about it before getting it tattooed."

Ellie does wait, for about a month, which in Ellie's world was the equivalent time as waiting a year. She books an appointment with the tattoo parlor and I wait at home with bated breath, hoping that she would have changed her mind after the consultation. I hear Ellie come through the apartment door and I get up to go see her.

When I look at her arm, I give a loud shriek. Her right arm is covered in tattoos! There is not a spot that isn't inked! She has a huge mermaid on her arm, along with an anchor, a seashell and the face of grumpy cat.

"What have you done Ellie!! I thought you were just going in for a consultation?!"

"I know...but I couldn't resist! Aren't they cool?"

"They are so big! Why did you get those ones? How would they match with anything that you wear? Your grumpy cat will forever clash with any designer outfit that you will wear!"

Ellie looks at me quietly while I am pulling out my hair in distress and bursts out laughing.

"Oh my God Cassie...your expression was priceless!"

I am still horrified but she continues, "Relax Cassie, it is just a tattoo sleeve that I am wearing. Did you really think I can get all of these tattoos done in an hour?"

I am relieved when I see Ellie pull away her tattoo sleeve and along with it her false tattoos, however, I see her wince a little and see that she has some redness on her inner wrist.

"Why is your wrist red?", I ask and go closer to inspect her forearm. There is a tattoo there! Ellie got a small tattoo on her inner wrist. It is a heart, just the outline, made by small red roses and black, spiky thorns. There is an infinity symbol extended across the middle of the heart outline, the color of ivy.

"You did get a tattoo! Does it hurt?"

"It stings a bit but the results are worth it. I really like how the design came out!"

"Is that the infinity symbol?"

"Yes...I am literally keeping this forever!"

"Roses and thorns?"

"Yes! I thought about it and this is what I really wanted to get inked."

"Why did you get the thorns? You could have made the design with just roses."

"Because it wouldn't have been real...life doesn't just come with roses. You get roses attached to the thorns or you get the thorns attached with the roses, depending on how you see it..."

"Wow...thinking about what you just said hurts my brain a little Ellie..."

"Do you like it Cassie? Think that I will regret it?"

"No...I think that you might keep it. It is pretty discrete and pretty...don't think it will clash with any of your outfits."

"Great! It has your approval....but after seeing your reaction, I might just get the grumpy cat tattoo!"

"Oh no you won't...don't you dare put me through that again!"

She just laughs at my horrified response. Ellie doesn't get a grumpy cat tattoo like she had teased me about but for my next birthday, she did get me a grumpy cat mug.

I would forever be reminded of her tattoo prank early each morning with grumpy cat frowning royally at me as I pour my

AISHA UROOJ

coffee in my mug.

Chapter Thirteen: Movie Night Fright

Once a month, Ellie and I have designated a movie night where we each take turns choosing a film for us to watch together. It is Ellie's turn to pick and she already has one in mind. Ellie wants us to see a horror movie and I am alarmed at her choice. I have to remind her why I think that it is such a bad idea.

"Don't you remember the last time we watched a scary movie? I couldn't sleep at all! I stayed up all night holding the frying pan in my hands."

"Yeah I remember, though I don't understand what you could have done with the frying pan...cooked a terrifying meal for your would-be murderer?"

"Ha ha very funny Ellie...and you can't make fun of my cooking anymore now that I can use the crock-pot!"

"Ok fair enough...but last time we watched a *psychological* thriller, this movie is a horror film. Most horror films look fake half of the time to begin with and their plots are very predictible."

"If you say so Ellie... but I am sitting close to you and if I get too frightened, you will have to turn the movie off."

"Fine it's a deal. Let's watch this...it will be fun!"

Ellie turns the light off and plays the movie while I sat close to her. Five minutes into the movie, I am still not having 'fun' and the gory scenes don't look fake but rather look very real to me, I grab Ellie's arm tightly and hold onto it. After thirty minutes or so, I become less jumpy and the movie gets interesting at this point. I hold my breath as the lead character is about to enter the dark basement alone but I feel Ellie move and reach for the remote. Apparently, Ellie doesn't feel the same about the movie because she turns it off and gets up to switch on the light.

"Why did you switch it off Ellie?", I ask. "Was the plot too predictable?"

"No it's not that....I can't feel my right arm anymore with you holding it so tightly," says Ellie, shaking off her numbed arm. "And besides, you scream like a banshee every five minutes. I can't have the neighbors think that I am murdering you."

"I can't help it if I am sensitive to sudden noise and murder scenes..", I say in a small voice.

"Nevermind...the movie was a little boring too. Let's watch something else that won't give you nightmares."

I am delighted when Ellie wants to see Audrey Hepburn's Breakfast at Tiffany's. We have watched this movie together so many times that we have the dialogues memorised and would say them before the characters do. I would often clean the apartment humming 'Moon River'. One thing is for sure, I will never ever get tired of watching it and I adore Audrey's portrayal as

Holly Golightly.

"Remember when we both dressed as a Audrey Hepburn movie character for the costume party? I was Holly Golightly and you were Eliza Doolittle from My Fair Lady?"

"Oh yes! It was so much fun speaking in that english accent. I think that I fooled almost everyone, they kept wanting to hear me talk more. They couldn't get enough of it."

"Hmmm I remember it a little differently. You wouldn't stop singing the 'Wouldn't It Be Loverly?' song in that ghastly accent. It drove everyone crazy!"

"Ha ha, whatever! I should do it again for the next party!"

"That wouldn't be very lovely..."

Ellie sticks her tongue out at my comment. We settle in to happily watch Breakfast at Tiffany's together. By the concluding scene, I am with tears in my eyes again despite having watched it before and Ellie sighs happily at the romantic final kiss. We both agree that it was such a good idea to stick with the classic movie.

"I want a cat named Cat", I say.

"I want a Paul Varjack! I want to be the rich lady and hire him for his services", says Ellie.

"I wonder what kind of books he wrote as a writer?"

"Probably about his life...or maybe a horror! You wouldn't be able to read it then..."

"You are going to keep teasing me about it, aren't you?"

"Yes, absolutely!"

We would end our disagreement with a pillow fight. I slept soundly that night, dreaming of Holly Golightly. In my dream, she finds and adopts a homeless puppy and names it puppy. I remember thinking that it was such an odd name for a pet and that I should ask Ellie about puppy names. I wake up the next morning with Moon River playing in my head again.

Chapter Fourteen: Flying High

My best friend Ellie is very particular about her diet, here she follows in the footsteps of her beauty idols, and just like her favorite actresses she doesn't drink a drop of alcohol nor rely on too much caffeine. In fact, she justs have one cup of coffee, with no sugar and a sprinkle of cinnamon in the morning.

I feel like I have sugar and caffeine coursing through my veins, but Ellie wouldn't even look at the seductive temptation that is a Iced mocha latte or caramel Macchiato with extra whipped cream. I would salivate and happily hand all my money and belongings over the aroma of freshly steamed milk, vanilla-flavored syrup with espresso and caramel drizzle, but Ellie says that she can live without the gallons of sugar found in the sinfully delicious concoction. Although I cannot emulate it myself, I admire her strength and her resolve to maintain a dewy complexion. Slowly at first, but already as a teenager, she started adding more healthy elements into her diet, things like more fruits and veggies and drinking plenty of water. She also decided to become a Vegan. In terms of exercise, she started going to weekly fitness classes on top of already running several miles on a daily basis. She doesn't like taking unneccessary painkillers or any other nonprescription medicines. She doesn't sleep late or sleep-in and wakes up early in the morning without an alarm. I marvel and am at awe of her superhuman resolve and dedication to her fitness.

We are both invited to go to a house party hosted by one of her actor friends at an upscale loft. When we reach there, there are around thirty or forty people in the modern space, which is decorated with hanging string lights and the atmosphere is casual, with soft music playing in the background. People are happily chatting away with drinks in hand or softly dancing to the chill-out lounge music.

Upon seeing the host, Ellie goes off to meet him and I surprised to see that she whispers something in his ear. Before the party, I didn't think that she knew him that well at all as she barely mentioned him. Her actor friend simply smiles and takes something out of his jacket and I see Ellie take something thst looks like a pill from his hand. He chats a bit more with Ellie then goes off to mingle with the other guests.

"Did you ask for an aspirin Ellie? You didn't tell me that you had a headache."

"No it wasn't an aspirin."

"What was it then? Tylenol or something, another painkiller?"

"It is a painkiller of sorts."

I am alarmed by her response. "What was it Ellie? Why did you take it?"

"It just something that helps to take the edge off. The host offered it and I didn't want to be a poor party guest so I took it. It is just a social thing, don't worry too much about it."

I am surprised at her nonchalance and want to say something...actually I am terrified for her and am shaking to the core. My knee jerk reaction is to shake some sense into her but I wait, trying to think of the best way to approach her about the seriousness of the situation.

I keep looking at Ellie during the party worried that she might collapse at any second but she doesn't seem to be any different, just more cheerful and relaxed than usual. She talks to a lot of people in the party and dances to the music for a long time. Ellie stays in her unnaturally happy mood but I worry about her getting dehydrated as she dances the night away with her unending energy. Finally, Ellie wants to leave the party and calls a taxi for us to head for home.

On our ride back home, Ellie looks at me and asks me why I had been so quiet. She prods me a few more time to speak.

"Say something Cassie..", she asks. "Is there anything wrong? Didn't you like the party?"

I feel that being honest would be the best approach. I pause before saying,"You upset me when I saw you take the drug Ellie. I am really worried for you."

"Is that all? It was no big deal Cassie. You shouldn't worry."

"It is a big deal, I wish you would understand Ellie. I don't want to see you dead. You don't know what there is in the drugs....you *can't* know, it is never safe!" As I say this, tears start to stream down my face and Ellie gets visibly upset seeing me cry.

"Oh geez Cassie, don't cry. You know I hate it when you cry. Please stop."

I can't stop the tears and I start to hiccup, Ellie quickly hands me a bottle of water and a tissue.

"Cassie, I promise I won't take any more drugs in parties...not even casually."

"You promise?"

"I swear!"

I wipe my tears and blow my nose into the tissue loudly which makes Ellie laugh. I feel glad that she made the promise and that nothing bad happened to her tonight.

"I love you Ellie. Please stay the smart, healthy Ellie that you are...you know the one that stops me from adding three teaspoons of sugar to my coffee?"

"More like four *tablespoons*. Ok Cassie, anything for you. Love you too", says Ellie and gives me a hug.

I am relieved when Ellie doesn't attend any more parties like the one before. That week, she goes back to her healthy routine and attends her fitness classes. It looks like everything has gone back to normal and the way it was before. She even stops me from adding the four tablespoons of sugar to my morning coffee, just like she had promised.

Chapter Fifteen: Fire Escape

I was heading for bed one night when I heard a noise coming from outside my bedroom window. We have the apartment building's fire escape attached just outside my bedroom window to use in case of fire emergencies, with an attached metal ladder that we could pull down to reach the ground safely. That also means, however, that anyone with enough ingenuity can also *climb* the said fire escape and have direct access to my window. Instantly images of masked robbers with sharp pointy knives and guns flashed before my eyes, I tried to calm my paranoia and suppress my irrational fears long enough to slowly peek out the locked window. *There was someone there!* I shriek and quickly get inside the blankets on my bed. Hearing my scream, Ellie rushes into my room with a frying pan in hand.

"What happened? Why did you scream Cassie?...and why are you shivering inside your blankets?"

"Th..There is someone hiding outside my window!"

Ellie heads toward the window. "Don't go there Ellie...it might be a m..murderer!"

"Cassie, the window is locked and I have this just in case", says Ellie pointing to the frying pan, her weapon of choice in this emergency.

Ellie looks out the window but then she starts to unlock the lock. "Ellie, why are you opening the lock?! He will come inside!"

"Relax Cassie...it is just a kid and he looks intoxicated."

I stop hiding inside my blankets and quickly go to the window to look at what Ellie was seeing and surely enough, it is a kid, age around eleven or twelve, sitting on the fire escape wearing only a thin white T-shirt and frayed jeans in the cold weather. He was shivering and smelled strongly of alcohol.

"Hey you, what are you doing here? We are going to call the police."

"Please don't call the police. My mom will kill me if she found out! I promised her I wouldn't touch Alex's stuff!"

He passes out after saying this. "Omg Cassie, he passed out! We need to get him inside and call the paramedics!"

I dial for an ambulance while Ellie drags the kid inside my room to save him from the cold and to check if he is breathing. The ginger-haired boy drifts in and out of consciousness but he is breathing. He wakes up again and looks at us confused.

"Where am I? Who are you... are you two angels? Did I die? Am I in heaven?"

I look at Ellie and am about to answer his question, but she speaks first. "Yes, we are angels but you are not in heaven yet."

I look at her surprised but she just winks at me. "Where am I then?"

"You have arrived at the gates of heaven but I am afraid you can't go any further."

"W..why not?"

"Well...it because you broke your promise to your mom"

"My mom?..."

"Yes your mom."

I look confused at Ellie. What was she doing?

"Did my mom found out? Did she cry? She cries when I don't listen to her. I am sorry mama...I didn't mean to make her cry."

"I..er..know your mom won't be happy when she finds out...but you can still make her happy and get into heaven, if you keep your promise to her."

"My promise?"

"Yes, your promise. We will be waiting for you by heaven's gates when you do."

"I will keep my promise, I promise!"

After saying this he passed out again but thankfully, the paramedics arrived at this point. We go to the hospital and wait to hear from the emergency doctor. The doctor tells us that the kid had alcohol poisoning but he was going to be ok and that a family member had been informed. A short time later, we see a ginger-haired man come rushing in and talk with the same doctor. The doctor points him to our direction.

"Are you the two girls who brought Samuel here? I am so sorry for the trouble he caused..but thank you for bringing him here!"

"Are you Alex?"

"Yes I am. How did you know?"

"Samuel mentioned your name before he passed out..he said that he wasn't suppose to touch your stuff."

"Yeah, I am his older brother. I kept some beer in my fridge but we had warned him not to touch it. Guess the warning wasn't enough. God...he scared us when he went missing. I am not going to keep any more drinks in the house."

"Please take good care of your brother", says Ellie. "He worries about letting down his mom. He seems like a sweet, loving kid."

"Thanks I will. Thanks again for bringing him here."

Alex exchanges contact information with us and we would periodically call him to check on Samuel.

A few weeks later, we receive a thank you card in the mail. It was from Alex thanking us for helping his little brother. He mentions that Samuel has changed since that day in the emergency room and no longer gets in any trouble. Alex says that his little brother doesn't want to break his promise to mom, saying that he had "two pretty angels waiting at Heaven's gates... who will let him in only when he keeps his promise."

Chapter Sixteen: Action Star

E llie has her first megahit movie, at the tender age of twenty, portraying a super cool action star.

For the role she does her own stunts and so she underwent an intensive and gruelling training in everything from knife-throwing lessons, boxing, archery and even riding a motorbike. Among the exercises, there was a "kidnap and rescue" portion. Ellie said that the trainers used live ammunition while "rescuing" Ellie from a staged kidnapping. Ellie said that live ammo was used to make it realistic to a hostile situation. She was also taught some outdoor survival skills, in case she finds herself in a life-or-death scenario in the wilderness.

Ha! I tell her that she has more to worry about city pigeons than the likelihood of that happening. Ellie said that the experience was all so exciting and wonderful...I really think she meant "physically and psychologically terrifying." Based on all that Ellie told me, the training seemed designed to frighten the life out of anyone, especially me.

Ellie wants me to go on a ride on the motorbike with her and I agree to but very reluctantly. I have second thoughts when Ellie arrives, looking intimidating and edgy in an all leather wardrobe, and when I look at the bike, which looks like it was built for speed. The expensive, sleek new bike must be a present from her parents. Ellie's parents are successful lawyers that work long hours and frequently have very busy schedules but they try to make up for their absences by buying anything that Ellie asks of them. Seeing my pale face, Ellie reassures me that it was perfectly safe to be on the bike. After much reassurance, I get on the bike with Ellie.

"Ellie, will you slow down! I don't want us to crash!"

"Cassie, I am already going below the speed limit, any slower and we would have to take a ride back home in the back of a police car."

I think about the possibility and am tempted by the thought of being in the nice and safe police car but since I don't want to get a criminal record, I pipe down my complains. I breathe out a big sigh of relief when we stop by a cafe to get some tea, mostly in order to soothe my frayed nerves. As Ellie parks her motorbike, we are approached by a tall, dark and handsome stranger.

"Excuse me, aren't you Eleanor James?"

"Yes I am."

"I am a big fan of your films! If you don't mind, can I get your autograph?"

"Sure, it will be my pleasure!"

As Ellie sign the autograph, her good looking fan looks towards me and asks,"Hi! Can I get your autograph too?"

"But I..I.. am not a movie star...", I stammer back to him, surprised at his request.

"What? No way!....I swear I saw you in a movie. I won't be surprised if you do, you are so beautiful." I blush.

Was he flirting? He gives me a wink and a stunning smile. I blush some more at his open flirting. He reaches for his pocket and brings out a card and hands it to me saying,"If you don't mind giving me a call sometime, here is my card with my phone number." He flashes a another killer smile and I stand there looking dumbfounded. At moments like these I wish I had something to save myself, like Penelope had her cloak to put off her suitors in the Odyssey. Thankfully, the handsome fan also has good manners to match his good looks and doesn't linger for long.

After he leaves, Ellie says,"Wow he was so charming! You should totally give him a call Cassie!"

"Ummm...I don't know..."

"Why? Why ever not Cassie? He was gorgeous!"

"...he was a little too.. perfect"

"Too *perfect*?!", says Ellie and laughs. "Most girls would die to go out with him!"

"But I am not most girls?"

Ellie shakes her head. "Oh Cassie, what am I going to do about you?"

"...you could get me a scone to go with my tea?", I ask hopefully.

"Well...as your unofficial official diet and sugar-intake monitor, I would have to stop you," says Ellie, but after seeing my face drop she adds,"but since you were just traumatized by my bike and by being asked out by a handsome, well-mannered stranger (you really are strange Cassie), as your best friend I will ask.....if you just want one scone or two to go with your tea?"

I am delighted with her offer and go with the more generous offer of two scones. I ended up eating one of Ellie's scones too but when she wasn't looking.

Riding back to the apartment, I am less nervous than I was before on the bike and feel exhilarated by the open air and breeze blowing in my hair. I can see why Ellie likes being on the bike so much and wanted to take me too, I had never felt so energized and free! I come back home happier about the world and feeling that anything was possible.

Life was an grand adventure and I was a part of it.

Chapter Seventeen: Wanderlust

Ellie received an around the world ticket from her parents for her twenty-first birthday and gets ready to pack her bags to go travelling. Her present is an all-expenses paid tour across much of the seven continents.

Ellie wants to go hiking in Austria, island hopping in Croatia, and talks about many many other locations on her bucket list. I, on the other hand, am more preoccupied thinking about her staying comfortable on the long plane journeys and tell her about the magical button found on most planes that would extend her sitting space.

"Ellie, do you know where this magical button is?"

"No where?"

"It is on the underside of the outer most armrest of the aisle seat, to find it, you slide your hand under the armrest, close to the hinge and feel for the button."

"What will happen when I press it?"

"Press it and you are now free to move that armrest up so it's flush with the back of your seat, giving you the freedom you deserve! A simple move and no more armrest digging into your side and a little swing room for your legs."

"Wow that is great to know!"

As I am busy chatting away about my little trick, Ellie looks at me fondly and says that she will miss me dearly on her trip. I know that she was only fascinated with anything that I talked about nowadays because I wouldn't see her for the next while. Also, because I was moving out and getting my own apartment while Ellie goes on her world tour.

We both know that we will miss each other dearly but I was excited that she was going on such a wonderful trip. Ellie was excited too that I was getting my own apartment. She said that she looked forward to seeing how I decorated my place after she comes back from her trip. She will see how I stay true to the minimalist lifestyle.

As Ellie is going on her trip, I think about the decision I had to make regarding myself. I had completed my high school diploma by taking online courses but I had been putting off making a decision about going to university I finally make my decision and break the news to Ellie.

"Ellie I am going to University..."

"University? How dare you! You betray me.."

"I am sorry Ellie! We made a promise to our parents to go for university if when weren't successful. You are travelling all year and I feel bored sitting at home. I can't keep working at the accounting firm, I will lose my mind there! I need to think about the future too."

"Ha! Cassie, you thought I was serious? I was just kidding! Of course you should go to University!"

"I should?"

"Yes...you need to put your big brain and creative energy to good use! You have deprived it for too long! I need you to explore beyond the apartment and your workplace, it is a big world out there Cassie, more wonderful and weird than you can imagine."

"I won't go to an expensive one, don't want my first year to be a financial killer or drain my savings."

"Where would you go?"

"There is one nearby offering a big scholarship package, along with access to a great first-year financial aid, meaning I wouldn't have to take time off to work, while still avoiding debt. I can also graduate earlier, which will also mean less cost."

"I am proud of you Cassie, you have learned a lot about finance from your job and you seem to have a well-thought out plan for handling University."

"I am glad you think so Ellie. Just don't ask me what my major is going to be. I don't know yet."

"We are taking baby steps here Cassie, not performing a miracle. I would have freaked out if you had already decided on the major too."

"You would have freaked out?"

"Yes, I might have even cancelled my trip to figure out what was wrong with you, conduct some tests to make sure you weren't an alien..."

"Hmmm...sounds about right! I would have gone to the doctor too to make sure."

We both laugh. Both of us are happy and excited for the journey ahead of us.

Chapter Eighteen: University

I decide to go for my university degree at an age when most of the university students would have been graduating, a fact that I felt acutely.

Sitting in my first university class, I feel both mature and very immature, a feat on its own, being able to feel both conflicting sentiments at the same time.

I look around at the classroom, there are around twenty or so students, happily chatting to each other, already formed as a close knit group. I sigh. It seems that only the professor standing in the front and myself hold the honor of being the most senior in the noisy young crowd. My attention is diverted to the front when the professor starts to write his name on the dry erase board.

He looks to be in his late-forties with sandy coloured hair and a sandy colored goatee to match, the goatee, however, is not the most prominent feature of his face. That honor would be given to his thick, black eyebrows.

I have never come across anyone with such distinguishing eyebrows! They seem to take a life of their own...thunderous and dark when the speaker was angry, and jovial and merry when the speaker was as such. I am still struck by the animation of expression in his eyebrows when the professor begins his lecture.

"As you can tell by my intelligent eyebrows that I am your professor for this class. You may address me as Professor Katzmarick or Professor K, if you are in a hurry. I am sure that you all think that I am here to teach you but you are wrong in that assumption."

There is a pause in the classroom as the students try to decipher what Professor Katzmarick had just said. Didn't he just say that he was the Professor in this class? What does he mean that he isn't going to teach us? The class look to each other with puzzled expressions.

"I can see that my comment has caused some confusion...excellent! it means you were listening....let me enlighten you as to what I meant. I am not here to teach you as much as you are here to learn. My 'teachings', as you may call it, would be useless if it falls to an unwilling ear and disinclined mind. If you are here to learn then perhaps my words may be of some use to you. Let me start by getting to know some of the reasons why you took this course...you can speak out loud, no need to raise your hand but do try to do it without talking over each other."

The students begin to cite their reasons for taking the class. Some liked the books in the syllabus, some took it because it was a prerequisite course for getting into the program that they wanted and some had heard that this course was creative and challenging but had a smaller course load than the other courses listed.

Professor Katzmarick listen to the reasons with interest with only his eyebrows giving away his train of thoughts. His eyes look across the students in the classroom and comes to rest at me. I barely have time to look away when he adresses me.

"Excuse me, you aren't a long lost daughter of mine by any chance or maybe one of the Katzmarick clan? I can see that your eyebrows could rival mine, perhaps not in command but at least in expression! Do you mind sharing you name? What is the reason for you taking this course?"

"Me? I..I..am Cassandra Grace. I took this course but... I am not sure why I did. I thought that if I took this class, I will figure out what I wanted."

"Ahhh...the paradox of choice! Fear not, yours is a valid reason.....having a plethora of choices can be overwhelming. Well Ms. Grace, thank you for *gracing* our presence!" The class groans at his joke but Professor Katzmarick continues, "My dear class, I have just started...you will have to anguish over my sense of humor for the rest of the semester. Coincidentally, when speaking of anguish and suffering, our first book up for discussion is Hamlet by Shakespeare."

Paradox of choice? Was that my problem...was Professor Katzmarick right? He had said that I had nothing to fear and that my indecision was still a valid reason to take a course. I hadn't thought that when I took this course that I would find any clarity in the fogginess that seemed my future path but sitting here in this class, I feel a strange connection to Professor Katzmarick disjointed, and some would say eccentric, manner of teaching. He continues to talk about Shakespeare.

"What is it about Shakespeare that still makes him relevant four hundred or so years later? Think about it...most contemporary works become outdated and forgotten over a short period of time but not his works. Why is that?"

A few students raise their hands to his question but Professor K continues on,

"Could it be that he touched the one area that would stay as important to us as it did to him? I am talking about human emotions...anguish, fear, love, hatred, revenge...you take your pick.

Why have I chosen Hamlet for you? I feel that his angst might speak to your own young conflicted souls. You might relish the complex agony in his soliloquys and think that Hamlet's internal dialogue could mimic the harshness of the internal critics in your own minds."

"Who am I to know?...perhaps you are at peace with your shortcomings in life and have no outer enemies to target for revenge? I would say this much, however, as long as you can feel the complexity of human emotions, it is still a relevant read for you. For your first assignment, I would like you to explore your own personal favorite emotion and write a page about it. I would expect this assignment due the next time I see you."

With these words, the class is dismissed, but I feel that it was too short of an introduction. Professor Katzmarick had raised so many questions, mostly about our own selves.

I think about the assignment that he gave us, what was my personal favorite emotion? What was something that I could write a page on? Would friendship be considered an emotion...did it fall under the umbrella of love? With these thoughts, I head for my next class feeling emotionally and mentally engaged and at least a little content being present at the place that people went to for higher learning.

Chapter Nineteen: Deciding on a Major

I sat thinking about the three witches from Macbeth (another Shakespearean pick by Professor Katzmarick), the one who are said to represent the three fates. Ellie catches me thinking.

"What are you thinking about Cassie?"

"How do you know that I was thinking about something?"

"You have your thinking face on."

"I have a thinking face?"

"Yes…and a sleepy face and a hungry face. So, what were you contemplating?"

"I was thinking about the three Fates. Have you ever thought about them?"

"No, I can honestly say I haven't and the only mythical creatures that I will be thinking about would be the Muses…you know since I am an aspiring actor wanting to be an inspiring one."

"That makes sense. I was wondering about which of the three Fates was the strongest. Clotho is the spinner of the thread, Lachesis is the allotter and Atropos is the inevitable, the one who cuts the thread of life."

"I would think that with a powerful moniker like the "inevitable" it would be Atropos?"

"True….but I was thinking it might be Lachesis? She is the one who decides how much time for life would be allowed for each person. If anyone can change a person's destiny it could be her since she has the ability to extend life."

"Interesting…what did your favorite professor say?"

"The same as you did. With a name like the inevitable and one who hands out death, Atropos is the clear winner."

"Ha! He agreed with me? I guess I could be a professor too. Come to think of it, Professor Ellie has a nice ring to it."

I laugh. "You will have a hard time being a professor Ellie."

"Why is that?"

"Because you will be too busy signing autographs for your students."

"I should be called Ellie the autograph signer then?"

"Maybe…Or you could become the newest Muse to be added to the lexicon?"

"Lexicon? Fancy university language there Cassie. It sounds like you are fitting right in."

I cant't help but smile at Ellie's words.

∞∞∞

During my first year at University, I take all the courses that I could manage in my syllabus in order to see what I would like. It was now time to come to a decision.

After much deliberation, I decide on my major and break the news to Ellie. She doesn't say anything but I do see her looking outside the window.

"What are you looking at?"

"Oh I was just looking at the sky."

"Why? Is something there?"

"No..not yet. The sky hasn't ripped open... there are no signs of any impending apocalypse. I didn't see a flying pig either but I just wanted to make sure. So you have finally decided huh?", Ellie says.

"You can stop looking for signs of impending calamity Ellie...I know I had been indecisive about it. My indecisiveness registering 10 on a scale of 1 to 10, but now I have chosen my major."

"That scale seems underrated."

"What scale would you use then?"

"More like you were indecisive on a scale of 1 to Hamlet."

"...that scale would work as well."

"So what did you choose?"

"I chose Hamlet."

"I mean what major you choose Cassie?"

"er...English Literature."

"That would make sense..so you going to be a writer then?"

"I haven't thought about that yet..."

Ellie sighs. "That makes sense too...I didn't expect you to have decided that yet." She looks out the window again.

"Ellie you can stop looking out the window, the sky will not fall just because I finally decide what I want to do with my life", I say laughing.

"It might!", says Ellie laughing too. "Congrats Cassie! Your favorite professor must be delighted at the news?"

"Yeah...he said I made a *major* decision choosing my major."

"He said that? Does he often make jokes like that...and still you chose English Lit?"

"It is not that bad...and I like it the most out of all my courses."

"I was just kidding Cassie. I see how your face lights up when you talk about it and how happy it makes you."

"It does make me happy", I say beaming.

"You finally find your *ikigai* Cassie?"

"What is that? Excuse me for being an ignoramus."

"It is a Japanese concept that roughly translates to 'finding your purpose' or 'a reason to get up in the morning'. *Iki* means life and *kai* is the realization of hopes and expectations. The theory is that by finding your ikigai and keeping busy with your purpose, you will enjoy a long and happy life."

"Wow that is beautiful Ellie. Maybe I have...hopefully I have.. maybe some day I will?"

"Ok Ok no need to solve all of life big questions in one day. We should celebrate this momentous occasion!"

Ellie takes us to a glamorous two-Michelin-starred restaurant with rooms inspired by the Salon de la Paix at the Palace of Versailles. The dishes were amazing and I am sure the bill was as well. Ellie hushes my concerns and says that good food and friendship are included in her ikigai, so we should live life and celebrate.

Chapter Twenty: A Book's Worth

I continue with the quest of reaching *minimalism nirvana* in my small apartment and go on a cleaning spree to get rid of things that I don't need. I go through boxes of boxes of things that I hadn't seen or touched since I left high school. In one of the boxes, I come across a book that I remember John had picked for me on our second date.

John takes me to a local bookstore in town and I am surprised to discover that it was my first time there. When I had wanted to borrow books, I would usually go to the school or public library. I must have missed seeing the small bookstore before because it was hidden behind an huge oak tree. There were so many books there, stuffed in every little corner and in no particular order, that it was hard for us to decide where to first start looking.

John comes up with the idea of looking for a book that we had already read before and to exchange it to one another. We spend some time browsing and we find what we were looking for.

"What book did you choose?"

"The Millionaire Next Door by Thomas J. Stanley and William D. Danko."

"Why do you want me to read it?", I ask looking at the book with interest.

"My father says that habits can make or break a person and that I should always aim for healthy habits in life. He says that I should read about successful people and learn from them. I had read this book for that reason."

Seeing John talk fondly of his dad makes me smile, "Your dad sound nice."

"Yeah he is great... he has made a lot of sacrifices for me and my siblings. I want to make him proud of me too."

I smile again and then look at the book,"What did you learn from this book? Did you like it?"

"I did like the book because it showed that anyone can become rich and that you don't have to be born wealthy to be successful in life, most successful people aren't."

I look at the back of the book and see that it is listed under 'Business & Investment' and as a must read for 'financial independence'. Since I have not heard those terms before, I am curious to learn more and to start reading the book.

"What book did you want me to read?", asks John.

"The secret garden."

"Isn't that a children's book?"

I blush at his question. "It was my favorite book when I was in elementary school."

"Your favorite? You must have really liked reading it then?"

"Yes I did!", I say happily. "It made me wish that I had a secret garden of my own to play with."

"What is the story about?"

"It is about a girl named Mary Lennox who is all alone in the novel at first but then she makes friends with kids her age and with some animals too." I find it hard to explain the themes in the book and to explain that the story is more than just being about children. I finally manage to say, "The story is about hope and happiness, that is why I like it so much."

The book shop owner had curiously been looking over while we were talking. He overheard our conversation because he comes to us with a smile and says, "Usually I don't get many kids in my bookstore and I like it that way. Forgive this old man for being biased and set in his ways but you two reminded me why I opened this store many years ago. I see myself in you both. I would like to give you two the books that you have in your hands. Don't refuse my gift as I insist. The books' cost are pennies next to their worth to you two as I am sure you will always cherish them."

I remember being surprised and blushing at his generosity, while John had graciously thanked him and accepted his gift gratefully. The shop owner had been right about the book's worth, I put my cleaning frenzy to a stop to make myself some tea and got set to reading the priceless gift once more.

Chapter Twenty-One: Innocence Defined

Ellie was fuming about a guy she turned down. I thought it was odd and not like Ellie to get so worked up over a guy asking her out.

Usually she is the one calming me down from an unexpected date offer. Ellie always takes it as a compliment when she gets asked out and even if she turns the offer down, she is sweet about it. I asked her what exactly caused her to be so annoyed. Ellie said a cute guy came up to her and started to compliment her. Things started out friendly and nice enough. He then asked her out and gave the reason *why* he was doing it. He asked her out on a date because he thought she looked really "pretty and innocent" to him. Ellie wanted to say yes but something didn't seemed right. She said that he didn't seem to take her hesitation well.

"Thanks for the compliment but if you don't mind, what did you meant when you said that I looked innocent?" He seemed confused by Ellie's question.

"I need to understand what innocence means to you. It is a reason why you are asking me on a date isn't it?"

"Yes it is sweetheart. You are all innocence."

"Can you explain what you mean? I know some guys say innocent when they really meant naive."

"You know...innocent..like trusting and such..."

"But I don't simply trust anyone blindly..."

"No I didn't mean gullible, you are smart...but you look innocent. It's a compliment, no need to overthink it. You are innocent, I know it."

"Well I haven't done anything that falls under a major bad...no cheating, theft, fraud, murder...so no, I am not guilty but I still don't know what defines innocence for you. I can ask you the same question, are you innocent? There isn't any police record that I need to worry about?"

Ellie said the last sentence laughing as she meant it as a joke but the guy started to sweat. He seemed shocked at Ellie actually having a backbone and he became especially shifty when she asked him that last particular question.

Turns out he was a fox trying to seduce her with flowery compliments. Ellie said that she was most surprised when he didn't have anything else to say when she asked him a few questions. He eventually made a run for it and she saw him cosying up to another girl not five minutes later calling his latest prey "cute and innocent".

"Good thing that you chased him off with your questions Ellie! You don't want to date a guy like that. He seemed so shady!"

"Yeah it's good I have a brain on me and went with my gut feelings. Hope no other girl falls for his tricks...trying to blindside with compliments and not telling anything about himself."

"He was right about you looking innocent though..."

"Really you too Cassie? It will drive me nuts...you have to tell me what that means??"

"You are all goodness my dear friend, you are like a light that attracts dark creatures. They better stay out of your way because you can totally kick their butts! Like a angel with ninja skills... criminals and fraudsters better beware!"

"Lol Cassie! You are too much..."

Chapter Twenty-Two: The Four Horsemen

E llie, at the age of twenty-two, is taking a break from dating right now she says in order to restore back her faith in love and man kind.

She has been in a few short-term relationships before and likes to affectionately refer to her ex-boyfriends as the four deadly horsemen. Each of the biblical four riders represent an element before the prophesied apocalypse, they are war, famine, pestilence and death. The horsemen in Ellie's relationship had similar characteristics.

Her first boyfriend came riding into her life on a figurative red horse. She was fourteen and the relationship lasted three weeks. They broke up over a video game as he wouldn't concede to being defeated by a girl. She grew tired of his combative nature and excessive competitiveness saying that it only ignited her own anger and bad mood.

Her second boyfriend she said was the rider on the black horse. She broke up with him at the age of seventeen because he wouldn't share his food with her. The last straw in the relationship was when she made sandwiches for both but he ended up eating everything unapologetically and leaving her hungry and famished. Ellie said that she wouldn't tolerate being with someone as selfish and greedy as him.

Her third boyfriend was after high school and at the age of nineteen. I didn't even get to meet him as Ellie found out through an incensed ex that he was a notorious cheater and had multiple 'girlfriends' at any given point. Within a month, he was sent riding away on his white horse out of Ellie's life for good. The cheat kept his player ways and continued to be a source of pestilence in the community.

I did get to meet her last boyfriend but I was surprised when they had broken up after only seven months. I ask Ellie if she had been unfair to him and to ask how he became the last of the four horseman.

"But Brad was nice...he was such a gentleman. He wasn't like any of your other boyfriends. Why did you break up with him Ellie?"

"It wasn't who he was, but rather what he did that made me break up with him."

"I don't understand. I met him a couple of times but he was always friendly. I can't imagine him doing anything bad to anyone."

"No technically he didn't mean to harm anyone...and I agree that he was perfect in every other way."

"Then why did you two break up? Why do you keep calling him Death on the pale horse?"

"Cassie....do you remember your conversations with him?

I think back to our conversation but don't remember anything unusual...except there was this one thing.

"Ellie, I do remember that there was this one weird thing...I kept sneezing whenever he talked. But that was me and not him..."

I remember when Ellie first introduced me to Brad, I kept interrupting our introduction by a series of sneezes. He could barely finish a sentence in front of me without interruption by a sneeze. Come to think of it, that happened every time that he came over.

"Cassie, that was part of the reason why I broke up with him.."

"So you broke up with him because you think I was allergic to him?", I ask confused.

"No dummy...you weren't allergic to him. He was a smoker and you kept sneezing because of the lingering smoke smell coming from his clothes."

Ah! Now it made sense..I am very allergic to any smoke and can't help but sneeze if it is in my vicinity. One of my many charms besides being hopelessly indecisive.

"His smoking was the dealbreaker? I think that he really liked you Ellie, he could have quit...Did you talk to him about it?"

"He had told me that he was a smoker on our first date but I didn't mind it at first because he was so cute. I thought that he would eventually give it up but he kept smoking cigarette after cigarette on our dates. I finally had to break up with him when all my food started to smell like cigarettes."

"That is a bummer. What a lousy habit to get stuck with. It is unfortunate, he could have been such a catch too..."

"Yeah I know but it was his decision to keep smoking. I had to decide what was best for me and my health as well.."

"I understand now Ellie that you didn't randomly break up with him. So are you still going to take a break from dating?"

"Yes...it will probably be for the best right now. I still have the memories of the four horseman to deter me from doing so at the moment, after that, I can't deal with a dating apocalypse!"

We both look at each other glumly, afterall, we were both warriors from the dating world with our own scars from the battles.

"Why is dating so hard Ellie?"

"I wish I knew Cassie, I wish I knew..."

"When will it get better?"

"I guess we will just have to sift through the bad to reach the good. Maybe a break isn't such a bad idea once in a while."

I see Ellie thinking deeply. I ask what she was thinking about.

"I have already named my ex-boyfriends after the four horseman. I was thinking what else could I name the new ones after? The seven deadly sins?"

"*Seven* deadly sins? Oh no Ellie, I hope you won't have to deal with a bad boyfriend ever again!"

"You are right...it is better to think positive. Amen to that!"

"Ellie, do you think there is such thing as the One?"

"Hmm...I know that some people believe in such things.."

"You sound pessimistic?"

"No, I am just tragically aware that people are people."

"And?"

"People are bags of emotions and feelings including frustration, annoyance and disappointment. It is too much to say someone is the One, unless you can be the One for them too."

"That makes sense. We shouldn't put all our hopes onto one idea or person unless we are willing to commit and sacrifice for them as well?"

"Or Cassie, we could just delude ourselves into thinking we are both the Ones and live happy til we die?"

"That could work as well."

We both look at each other and smile at our conclusion.

Truth be told, no matter what Ellie says, she is a hopeless romantic at heart and after her break from dating, she will be back to her optimistic self again. Her heart is too big for setbacks or resentments when it comes to finding love.

Chapter Twenty-Three: Lovesong

Ellie has been all over the news lately. She attended a awards ceremony held somewhere in Europe. She looks ethereal in her fitted light blue gown with her golden hair done in soft waves. It had been raining that day, making it slippery condition for high heels. I had gasped when I saw Ellie slip on live TV....right into the arms of a handsome attendee!

A *very* desired and eligible someone.

It turns out Ellie was in the enviable position of falling in the well-defined arms of the biggest K-Pop singer in the world.

The press goes wild! The picture is featured in all the entertainment magazines. I see Ellie apologize profusely to the singing sensation for her misstep, he looks a bit dazed...but was he angry? It is hard to read his expression. I want to reach out and give poor Ellie a hug!

We would later find out that the singer had actually been instantly smitten with Ellie! Soon after his fateful encounter with our golden heroine, he writes a romantic ballad and it becomes his biggest hit. In the song, he croons about meeting a falling angel one rainy day and the song is titled "Eleanor." Ellie had inspired her very own romantic lovesong!

My empty heart and lonely eyes

Searches you in the open skies

For your name I had been calling

My beautiful angel you had been falling

Raindrops, raindrops from the sky

Heart pounds, heart breaks, and I cry

Eleanor, my love how far have you come?

To see me from the heavens above

Eleanor, sweet angel how far have you come?

To embrace me from the heavens above....

I walk in the room to see Ellie dancing to the same melody. She freezes when she sees me. She has a guilty expression, like she had been caught red-handed.

"Ellie, what are you doing?"

"What?"

I raise one eyebrow at her. "What song are you playing?"

"Oh it's nothing..."

I squint my eyes at her lie.

"Why are you looking at me like that?"

"You know he wrote that song about you."

"Yes I know, but I can't help myself......it is just so catchy!"

I just shake my head. Despite Mr. Handsome singer's love song and romantic overtures, Ellie remains dedicated to her acting pursuits which is a little ironic and hypocritical of her considering how much she wants me to date and find Mr. Right!

Ellie often makes fun of me and my (imaginary) list of requirements for my potential dates. She makes it seem like I am super picky. She would pretend to be me, shaking her head in disapproval and ticking off her fingers, "Too loud. Too creepy. Too smelly. Too perfect. *Too* weird."

When she sees that I don't stop her, she would continue with the exaggeration, "I want someone who *gets* me. Someone who likes icecream in any weather, but *especially* in winter and when he has the flu. Someone who likes to listen and someone who likes to talk, preferably does *both* at the same time. Sensitive but strong. Deep and brawny. A strong, silent but *social* type."

On and on she would go dramatically: "He shouldn't live too near as that would be too convenient, He shouldn't live too far as that would be inconvenient, etc etc"

As she seems to enjoy her creative little monologues I don't correct her, but personally, I think that she is wrong and being silly about the situation. Despite what she says, I would say I am pretty open-minded. I do have only one major requirement though, above anything else, I don't want to date anyone named John.

"What if it is *your* John?"

"What do you mean?", I say blushing and trying not to think back to John Damon from high school.

"What if John comes looking for you? You wont send him away and ignore him again."

"You make me sound like a heart-breaker!"

"You didn't answer back his texts."

"I was sixteen!........I didn't know any better," I say sheepishly.

"So you admit you did him wrong! Now that you know better, you won't do it again?"

"What if he doesn't come back?"

"What if he does?"

"What if he doesn't remember me?"

"What if he did?"

I can see that Ellie won't let the topic go and my brain starts to get tired of the hypothetical situation, exasperated I say, "If John comes back, I will never send him away."

"You promise Cassie?"

"Yes, yes I promise!......but til that happens, I don't want to date anyone named *John*."

Ellie laughs, "I feel sorry for Johns everywhere."

"Maybe they are the lucky ones", I mutter darkly.

Chapter Twenty-Four: Blind Date

I am set up for a blind date by a well-meaning neighbor, who says that she has the perfect match for me.

As I head towards my date, Ellie reassures me that she will bail me out if things don't go well. I reach the restaurant to see a guy who could be mistaken for a Abercrombie model, dressed impeccably, waiting by the front doors. As he is already on time and waiting for me with a pleasant smile, I feel that the date would go well and that I was unnecessarily worried about calling Ellie for help. As the date progresses, however, my blind setup starts to fall under the category of "too weird."

"So...I will tell you upfront that I am looking for the *one*," my blind date says looking at me expectedly. "I am a very faithful person and I want to spend the rest of my life with that special someone. I want to wake up every morning next to the special lady by my side."

"That sounds lovely...what kind of person are you looking for?"

"Good question, I can see that you are very smart! I am looking for someone like me...you know confident, open-minded and..of course, someone as pretty as you. I have never met a girl as pretty as you Cassandra!"

"Please..c..call..call me Cassie", I stammer, suddenly feeling very self-conscious after his bold compliment.

"So you stammer? How cute! If you stay with me I promise that you will never stammer again...I have that effect on people you know? I think I they look up to me seeing my confidence and success as quite a remarkable entrepreneur. I inspire them for sure! You know there was a time when I had solved......."

My blind date continues talking about his talents but I am taken aback by what he had said. Suddenly I remember a conversation I had with John, then I had also inadvertently stammered on our date.

"I am s..sorry John, sometimes I s..stammer when I get n..nervous...", I say embarrassed.

"Please Cassie, I wish you wouldn't apologize for that. It isn't anything to be embarassed about. You are not alone, many people have difficulty with speech...I did too. You have such original thoughts and ideas, that I would truly grieve to miss out on, if you felt too embarrassed or shy to say them."

Normally, I would blush and become quiet at such a compliment but John had said it so genuinely and earnestly that I felt better after him having said it.

"So you had t..trouble with s..s..stammering too John? How did it s..stop?"

"I was a shy kid and had trouble talking to anyone. My parents were very supportive though and would never put pressure on me to be more social. I remember that they got me a dog for my seventh birthday and I simply loved him. I would spend hours talking to him and he became my best friend. I became more social as I took him for walks and more people approached me.

After my siblings were born, I became a big brother and felt more responsible. I became confident in my interactions with others..so I guess, the stammering just went away. I still feel it come up sometimes, when I am nervous but I remind myself that being self-conscious about it will only make it worse...so I try to relax myself and try to find the best outlook on the situation. I admit that it takes work...but I never regret, and am grateful, to be able to share my thoughts with others with more ease than I could when I was a kid..."

What a big difference, I think, between John's response to my stammering to my current date's, who is sitting across from me chatting away animately.

I barely respond to him but he is satisfied by my nodding. I have spoken three words total in our conversation but he doesn't notice and continues talking. I am jolted back to the present when my blind date asks me a direct question. I was so lost in that memory of John that I hadn't realized that the conversation with my blind date had taken an alarming route. I finally realize what exactly my blind date had just asked of me.

"So...do you want to go home with me? Normally, I would never ask this from a first date as that would be very improper....but I feel a connection with you that I feel that I must explore further! I can't let you go without knowing you more closely. You are just so mysterious Cassandra! I feel such a connection with you that I hadn't felt with anyone before!"

'Oh my God! What do I do now? What do I say?!', I think to myself.

I start to panic and in doing so, I spill my drink on my dress. Seizing on my accident as an divinely given opportunity to get away from the conversation, I excuse myself to the ladies room to get cleaned up and once in the washroom, I send out an emergency SOS text to Ellie.

'Help me Ellie!!' I text to Ellie and like the darling angel that she

AISHA UROOJ

is, she immediately texts back that she was on her way.

I wait a while longer however I can't stay much longer in the washroom without my date getting suspicious so I return very slowly back to our table.

He seems glad to see me back and this time he proceeds boldly by holding my hands. I am about to pass out in my anxiety but then I hear a commotion in the restaurant. People are talking loudly, suddenly more animated and there is an excitement in the air as a big Hollywood star has arrived in the very same restaurant.

"It's Eleanor James!", the restaurant patrons whisper excitedly.

'Oh thank God for Ellie!', I think. Even my blind date is distracted by the noise and he excuses himself and asks me to come with him to see what the excitement is about. He informs me that he is a fan of Ellie and that he would like to get her autograph. As we reach her table, I see him ruffling his hair and setting his tie straight.

"Excuse me Ms. Eleanor James? I am your biggest fan... What an honor to meet you! I have to say that I have never met a girl as pretty as you!! You are such a bold actor, so very confident, just like me..."

I had to stop myself from laughing at his false gallantry. My blind date had said to Ellie what he had minutes earlier already professed to me.

I had been feeling bad about leaving him during our date but now I saw his distraction to Ellie as the chance to head for home unimpeded. He barely listens to me when I say that I had to leave early and say goodbye. He continues to talk to Ellie while I head out the restaurant and grab a taxi.

Later, Ellie would tell me that my blind date had invited her to his apartment as well, saying that he never said that to anyone before at a first meeting. Ellie had called security at that point and my blind date had been escorted out the restaurant by the two burly bodyguards. He did text me a few times the following day saying that he was sorry that our date had been cut so short and that he wanted to get to know me better by having another date. I had politely declined another meeting and had thanked Ellie a million times for coming to my quick rescue.

Chapter Twenty-Five: Opposites in Nature

E llie remains my emergency rescue for bad dates but soon she too becomes swamped by several new acting projects.

As the time between Ellie's visits get longer due to her hectic schedule and I have trouble falling in love with anyone, I decide that I needed some furry companionship. I tell Ellie of my decision to get a puppy. I should have kept my ears away from the phone as I knew she would squeal...and she does loudly.

As my ears recover, she asks: "Cassie, can we pick the puppy together?"

"Of course we will!", My comment sets off another burst of happy noise from Ellie.

The next time she drops by, we go together to the animal shelter to find the perfect furry match. While we are looking at the many wonderful dogs, the puppy saw her before she did.

It was love at first sight! He barks happily to draw our attention and furiously began to wag his golden tail.

"Oh how adorable! Look at how happy he is to see us...Cassie we should get this cutie!"

"He is pretty cute. Ok...I will go sign the papers. What should we name him?"

"We should name him Buddy," says Ellie.

"Buddy? Just Buddy...Why Buddy?"

"Isn't that why you are getting him?"

"So...it should be Buddy?" I look at the dog as if to ask him what his thoughts were on the name being chosen for him. He simply blinks his brown eyes in response.

It must have been the matching golden hairs but I swear "Buddy" loves Ellie more than me. For a moment, my green eyes get greener with envy but then I think that any dog who adores Ellie can't be bad. After this quick assessment, he easily passes my un-scientific dog personality and compatibility test.

Buddy, the three-month old golden retriever, joined Casa Cassie with the blessing of his favourite person Ellie.

I should have known that my dog would turn out to be my polar opposite. He likes walks. He likes early mornings. He likes walks on early mornings, both together! Let me tell you that I am definitely not a morning person....and I am a total couch potato.

I complain about my dilemma to Ellie who is not listening to a word I said.

"But Ellie...my university class doesn't start til ten but he wakes up at 6am and starts barking at me! He wants to go outside even when it is freezing!"

"Buddy is adorable!"

"Didn't you listen to a word I said? He turns into a aggressive little furball if I don't take him on his walks!"

"You need the exercise Cassie, being sedentary is not good for your health."

I forgot that I was talking to Ellie, the fitness fiend. She would extoll me the virtues of fitness. She would throw me words like HIIT, Crossfit, Crunches, Pliometrics, Cardio, Planks, Burpees and God-knows-what other forms of physical torture and pain disguised as exercises. I give up explaining my plight to Ellie and dutifully set my alarm for my early mornings.

I do try to wake up.

I miss the alarm again and I hear Buddy barking angrily at my deception and broken promise.

I groan... but I find it odd that he barks only for five more minutes. Curious, I peek out of my blanket to see both Buddy and Ellie by my bedside, looking at me.

Ellie came to my rescue! She is geared up for jogging in her cool workout clothes and blond ponytail in a cap, ready to go. She must have arrived early and opened my apartment door with the spare key.

No wonder Buddy had gone quiet! I had been spared his tiny wrath!

I leave the two morning people and puppy to enjoy their walks, while I remain snuggled and warm in my bed.

Ellie would help me out a couple of times whenever she was in the city and Buddy would wait for her faithfully by the front door rather than to start barking at me early in the morning. It is more than enough for me and I am grateful as I at least get a few days where I can sleep in!

Thank the lord for sweet, merciful Ellie!

Despite our different preferences when it comes to exercise, I think that Buddy is a great listener.

Ellie's eyes would start to glaze over sometimes but Buddy would never get tired of listening. No matter what I talk about, he is always responsive. My newest interest is financial blogs. Investments or money wasn't something that my parents talked about nor was it taught in high school. I have always been, as they say, financially prudent whereas Ellie is more carefree about her expenses. Now that I have to work within a budget, I discovered the FIRE community online and it is all I can talk about.

"Ellie, did you know that FIRE stands for Financial Independence, Retire Early?"

"That is interesting..."

"Yes, we should go over our budget together and see where we can save more for retirement!"

"It is too early to think about retirement and besides, my budget is making more money and then spending it."

"Hmmm... did you know what the book *The Richest Man in Babylon* would say about that: A man's wealth is not in the purse he carries. A fat purse quickly empties if there be no golden stream to refill it."

"Fat purse empty...got it...I will try to remember that..."

"Did you know that lottery winners lose most of their money within a few years because they don't know how to manage it properly?"

"If I win the lottery, I will get myself a financial manager."

"But Ellie, you should learn about managing money yourself. It is an important life skill!"

"Cassie, I just remember about something urgent. I will see you later. Bye!"

I pout when I see Ellie disappear. She often remembers about something 'urgent' when I start to talk about budgets.

Sigh.

When I have the same conversation with Buddy, on the other hand, he never gets tired of it and he gives the perfect responses.

"Buddy can you believe the MER ratio on some of these mutual funds!"

Buddy growls angrily.

"I know right! ETFs are so much more reasonable when it come to MERs."

Buddy wags his tail in approval.

"Buddy, Roth IRA or Roth 401k, what do you think?"

Buddy tilts his head thoughtfully.

"Buddy, don't you love automatic savings and investing? It makes saving money so much easier and convenient!"

Buddy barks in excitement.

I am so glad he listens well. I feel myself swell with pride at having such a smart dog as my financial collaborator. I am so happy with his responses that I give him a much deserved hug and say, "I love you my smart little furball, you are my Financial Puppy Guru Buddy!".

Buddy licks my face happily.

Buddy and I may have our differences but at least we are on the same wavelength when it comes to financial matters and saving for our future.

One day, I will convince Ellie as well but til that day, I will keep the financial conversations between myself and Buddy.

Chapter Twenty-Six: Fame is a Dangerous Drug

Ellie has been in a funk lately and I am worried about her. She is devastated that she lost out a role to another actress because the director thought she was too pretty for the character and despite her best efforts, he doesn't take Ellie seriously enough. What is worse is that her latest movie did poorly in ratings and she is not being called back for any other roles.

She spends countless hours on her phone obsessing about comments on social media and it is making her more and more depressed. I myself am a social media hermit, so besides texting and video calls, tend to stay away from those sites. I try my best to understand her obsession and to console her but she is starting to lose sight of herself and her love of performing. I fear that her obsession is spiralling into something darker.

"Oh my God Cassie, have you read what this fan said on twitter?

He said that I was better off modeling as I don't have it in me to act."

"That is harsh and it is not true Ellie, you are very talented. Remember what our theatre teacher has said about your school play? He said that he had never seen such natural talent."

Ellie nods but doesn't seem convinced by my answer. She looks back at her phone.

"Cassie another 100 people unfollowed me and I am not getting as many likes as when I was in that superhero movie."

"You don't know these people Ellie. It doesn't matter if they don't give as many likes as before, that doesn't mean anything anyway."

Ellie is still not listening and looks dejectedly at her phone.

"Did you read what this critic said about my new movie? She says that she wants her money back and wants me to apologize for wasting two hours of her life!"

I shake my head, "Some people just delight in being a troll and being mean. Don't pay any attention to them."

Ellie finds another comment that makes her miserable and I decide that I had had enough of this.

"Ellie it is time that you step away from your phone. You are spending too much time reading about negative comments from people that don't know you and it is making you lose sight of yourself. You are very talented and you never need to apologize to anyone about your work. You are just experiencing a gap in finding the right role for you and believe me when I say this, when you find it and you will, you will be unstoppable and these same people will be clamoring for your attention!"

Ellie seems to hear me this time and puts her phone away. She spends much less time reading comments on social media and her mood slowly gets better. In her sad state, she had made herself isolated from the world and had stopped doing the things that she enjoyed.

She goes back to making time for her hobbies, begins to focus on fitness and other social activities again. Buddy also helps her feel better by going with her on her long walks.

Weeks later, she gets a phone call about a potential movie role. She goes to the audition and is selected for the lead. It is the most challenging role in her entire career! She has a serious character, like she had wanted, and it is of a recovering alcoholic, an orphan, who is trying to get rid of her addiction in order to gain custody of the only person she has in the world, her 11-year old sibling. The story shows the struggles of a determined older sister that wants to protect her younger sister while battling her own inner demons.

Her newest movie is a sleeper hit, earning rave reviews worldwide and she receives an oscar nomination for her moving performance.

When I first see the movie I am terrified to look at Ellie's character as she looks gaunt. She lost a lot of weight for the role and looks frail and dejected. I have never cried so much as I did during that movie. I am astonished at the depth that Ellie portrays. She is unrecognizable as the different sides of her character and I was truly frightened when she smashes bottles of alcohol in rage, having never see her be angry before. After the movie ends, I rush towards Ellie and give her a huge hug.

"Cassie, are you crying?"

"Ellie I don't know what to say. I never want to see you like that again!"

"It was only a movie Cassie and I was playing a character."

"Yeah you frightened me a little. I never knew that you could be angry!"

"Yeah this role pushed my boundaries. I had to go to a dark place and explore this character's motivations, fears, weaknesses and then strengths. It really took a toll on me but I am happy with the performance....but an oscar? I wasn't expecting that!"

"I am so happy for you Ellie, you deserve it. You were truly amazing!"

"Thanks Cassie. Thanks for helping me see the big picture when I was feeling down."

"Any time for you Ellie and if you ever feel like smashing your phone, I will do it for you!"

Ellie laughs at this. "Oh my God Cassie, I have been nominated for an oscar...AN OSCAR!"

"Yeah! But what are you going to wear?!"

We both look at each other and laugh. Buddy barks excitedly as well. Ellie's fame goes into superstardom after this role and she never has to worry about finding work again.

Her critics can't find one single bad thing to say about her movie portrayal. As for the critic who wanted her money back, she sends a letter of apology to Ellie and asks her to come give an interview for her column. Ellie, being the sweet person that she is, accepts her apology without any hesitation and obliges her critic-turned-fan with an in-person interview.

Chapter Twenty-Seven: Reach Beyond the Stratosphere

E llie has been doing great in her career. She is getting requests for appearances at all the major talk shows, but out of all of them, Ellie truly shines at her appearance on the Ellen show.

For the show, she wears a cute black and white polka-dot dress with white sneakers and her hair is made into a ponytail. It is my favourite interview of her as she is affable, charming and comes across as lovely as her real self and offscreen persona.

"Eleanor James, thank you for joining the show today."

"Wow Ellen, thank you for having me. Please call me Ellie, all my friends do and the honor is all mine Ellen. I am a great fan of your show."

"That is nice of you to say Ellie. I must say that you are even more beautiful in person and that the pictures don't do you justice."

"Thank you Ellen, I agree."

"Wow, you agree? that is a first...most guests would instead choose to be modest about it."

"I am nothing if honest", says Ellie laughing. "Don't get me wrong, I am truly flattered by your compliment Ellen even though I don't always feel beautiful without the fancy gowns, my makeup team and sparkling accessories....and often I wish that I wasn't so skinny and had some curves! What I meant to say is that I agree that the pictures don't do me justice, more specifically don't do my freckles justice."

"Your freckles?"

"Yes! I take great pride in my freckles, especially the ones on the corner of my right cheek that forms the pattern of a small heart. Most photographers dont capture them in all their glory or edit them out, focusing on my eyes instead."

"You know they say that the eyes are the windows to the soul?"

"That is a beautiful expression Ellen. I wish they made one for freckles as well, they seem to be neglected by the poets!"

"Perhaps I could try, something like Ellie's freckles are windows to the heart?"

Ellen, Ellie and the audience all laugh.

"Let's talk a little bit more about you, something that we won't learn from pictures, what would you say is your best quality?"

"I would say that my best quality is that I can be stubborn."

"How is that your best quality?"

"I don't give up easily and usually get what I set my mind on to achieve."

"That's great, good on you. Setting your mind on something and then achieving it is a great quality to have. Let's talk about what you feel is your worst quality and why do you think that is?"

"I would say that my worst quality is that I am stubborn and that I usually get what I want because of it", says Ellie coyly.

Ellen and the audience laughs.

"It's complicated then? Your best, and worst, qualities it seems have led you to amazing successes so far. An oscar nomination, every other awards that you can think of BAFTA, SAG, Emmy and even a Grammy, even though indirectly. You were the inspiration behind an grammy winning song as well?"

"Yes I have heard about that. I can't take all the credit though...I owe it all to my graceful ability to walk in high heels on slippery rainy days and to my luck in finding the right person to stumble onto accidentally", says Ellie laughing.

"Perfect way to become the year's most viral meme as well. So what future projects do you have planned? Where have you have set your sights and heels for next?"

"I have worked in so many beautiful and dreamy locations: France, Thailand, Spain, Japan...I want to do one movie on the next new horizon for mankind, on the red planet of Mars."

"*Mars*? You know that would only be a one-way ticket. I would miss you if you left, I think that we all will", says Ellen looking at the audience. The audience agrees.

"Yes, that would be a grand adventure! Who knows? I might convince some aliens to give me a ride back to Earth", jokes Ellie.

"Well, you certainly are stubborn enough and beautiful enough to convince them. You have *me* convinced and become your fan Ellie. I look forward to seeing your next movies and the one at Mars! Do come back to the show again, I would love to continue our conversation", says Ellen. The audience are in agreement and applause well for Ellie.

Ellie laughs wholeheartedly and thanks Ellen. After the show, Ellie tells me that her appearance on the show was a dream

come true for her. I felt so happy for Ellie, she deserves this recognition and so much more. I feel proud to be her friend and my
heart wishes for her to achieve everything that she desires.

Chapter Twenty-Eight: Oscar Night

E llie's mom invites me to watch the Oscars together with her at her home, as Mr. James is away on a seminar and all her friends are busy hosting their own soirees.

Ellie's parents live in a gorgeous French Normandy-style mansion, just on the outskirts of the city, nestled at the end of a quiet cul-de-sac As we sit in the two-story living room, I observe the various antiques and figurines displayed on the marble fireplace but note that they aren't any family pictures on display. I would have liked to see childhood pictures of Ellie and her with her parents but perhaps, I muse, the designer didn't think that it would fit in with the interior design?

I feel that the magnificent house and its exquisite interior decor does display the elegance and glamor fitting for movie star Eleanor James.

"You have a beautiful home, Mrs. James. Ellie must love it here, it is so much like her style"

"Thanks dear, it is sweet of you to say. Eleanor used to love it here too, but now she thinks that it is too opulent and that it doesn't feel homey enough."

I am a little surprised to hear that Ellie had said that, she loves staying at her parent's house whenever she has time to do so, perhaps she hadn't been in a good mood when she said it? Not knowing what to say, I reach for a glass of water.

"Eleanor is finally at the Oscars, my little darling is so deserving! She has worked hard to be where she is, many just see her priv-ileged upbringing and think that it is all handed down to her! Most people don't understand the sacrifices she has made for her career, that is why I only wanted to have you here with me today dear as I know you understand, being her close friend. She is always working, doesn't even spend time on anything else. She says that she doesn't want to date right now, that it becomes a distraction. Can you believe her? You are her best friend, can you talk to her and convince her to date someone?"

I nearly choke on my sparkling water. Apparently Mrs. James thinks that I can help Ellie with her love life and doesn't know that my own dating endeavors are much like a slow-moving trainwreck. I can see that she is concerned for her daughter and means well, I also don't want to hurt her feelings or dash her hopes and trust in me, so I do the only thing that I could in such a situation and I lie.

"I will convince Ellie to slow things down and to give dating a chance, I am her best friend so she will listen to me. I am great at meeting new people and match-making, I will do what I can to help Mrs. James. Don't worry!"

She seems satisfied with my reply and I am relieved that she doesn't ask me any more questions about my imaginary match-making successes. The Oscars are being televised live from the red carpet and we see Ellie come onscreen.

She is dazzling in her plunging black gown with a dramatic train that highlights her tall, svelte body. She has sultry smokey cat eye and her hair is made into an elegant chignon, which displays off her very beautiful sapphire and diamond earrings as well. She has on diamond rings and diamond cuff bracelets as well but none are as striking as her earrings. The dark blue Burmese sapphires in the diamond pendant earrings are the same colour as Ellie's eyes and almost as radiant.

Ellie had mentioned that the sapphires are one-of-kind due to their large size and that she was borrowing all her diamond accessories from a famous jewellery designer. The beautiful sapphires in the earrings alone were worth in the several millions!

We see many more stars arrive at the red carpet, they spend a few minutes interviewing with the entertainment reporters and correspondents, and then quickly move inside the theatre where the award ceremony is being held.

When it comes time for the Best Actress in a movie category, both Mrs. James and I hold our breaths. It is a tough category to compete in this year as there are many terrific talents nominated for the leading lady roles. My heart pounds faster and faster when the hosts bring out the envelope to announce the winner, "And the winner for Best Actress is..." *not* Ellie, I realize severely disappointed. Mrs. James and I both have our jaws drop in disbelief, but unlike the two of us, Ellie's demeanor stays the same and she graciously claps for the winner without any hint of disappointment.

"She has been robbed!", cries Mrs. James.

"I agree! Poor Ellie, I hope that she is not too disappointment about not winning."

Both Mrs. James and I call Ellie on her phone to commiserate with her about her loss but she seems to be handling the situation much better than we were.

"Don't worry you too, I am ok. I didn't think I would win it this year, the competition was just too amazing. I am amazed that I was even *considered* with the other nominees. I will just have to try harder next time...but I am happy with the recognition that I got from this nomination, it gives me even more incentive to keep trying. I will win a Oscar, you will see...it just wasn't meant to be this time."

Both her mom and I want to give Ellie a hug over the phone for putting on such a brave face. We want to talk to Ellie some more but she says that she has to leave soon and head towards a post-oscar party. Mrs. James and I continue to talk to each other about what happened and what we thought about the show, but as I had Buddy waiting for me, I made to leave as well. I reach home sadly, feeling letdown from the night.

I wake up at 3am in the morning when I hear my phone ringing by my bedside. Half-asleep I wonder who it could be and see that Ellie has been calling me.

"Cassie I lost it! I don't know what to do!"

Poor Ellie, I think, she has finally realized that she lost and is taking it hard.

"It is ok sweetie, you can win next year. Don't be sad."

"Cassie but I lost it! I can't find it anywhere!"

I am a little puzzled at her conversation. She sounds like she was panicking about something. I quickly realize that Ellie had been talking about losing one of her earrings. Her very expensive borrowed earrings!

"When did you notice that your earring was missing? Have you traced back your steps?"

"No I haven't traced back my steps. I was panicking so much that I didn't know what to do so I called you. That is a good idea Cassie, I will go back the way I came."

Ellie continues her search, telling me the locations as she went.

"Cassie, I can't find the earring anywhere, it might be lost or stolen by now. I...."

She pauses for such a long time that I think that the phone has been disconnected. I keep calling her name but she doesn't say anything. She finally comes back on the phone and she sounds delighted, "Cassie I got the earring back and you won't believe how!"

I am relieved to hear that she is safe and sound and that she has found the earring, "Ellie, you scared me when you went quiet. I am glad that you found them! Where did you find it?"

"Cassie, I didn't find them, someone else did. You won't believe who though...it was James...James 'hottie' Evans. It gets better too, he asked me out on a date!"

James Evans? *The James Evans* that Ellie has had the biggest crush on? I couldn't believe my ears! Ellie sounds ecstatic about meeting her dream crush and I am so happy that her night turned out better than how it had started.

Ellie's changed luck continues the next morning, when she is voted best dressed by all the fashion experts. I am amused when the experts rave about her choice of earrings.

Her date with James Evans would also make front-page news in the entertainment magazines. James Evans and Eleanor James make the hottest couple in the entire planet. The "James-es" as their shippers or fans call them are all that anyone is talking about. All of the fans are hyperventilating and the world goes mad over the news of their pairing.

I receive a phone call from Ellie's mom thanking me for thinking about Ellie and for setting up her date with James Evans. Apparently, Mrs. James thinks that I was the matchmaker behind the date!

Despite my protests to the contrary, she continues to thank me for being such a good matchmaker and I give up trying to convince her otherwise, remembering that I was the one who had initiated the white lie.

Mrs. James remains convinced to this day that I was the one who introduced Ellie to her dream date and praises my matchmaking expertise to anyone that she meets.

Chapter Twenty-Nine: A Reporter's Favor

After Ellie is seen with James Evans, on her now famous date, the paparazzi have made day-to-day living a nightmare for Ellie.

She can't leave her apartment without being mobbed by a throng of tabloid reporters flashing their cameras and taking her pictures. As soon as she is spotted, the paparazzi gather round her and ask her a stream of questions regarding her date and yell very personal questions about her love life.

At first Ellie was amused by their attention but more and more she started to get frustrated when it would interfere with her daily chores. She misses going for a afternoon run and can't even leave her apartment to come see me. She is starting to feel like a prisoner in her own building. I decide that I should save her some agony and go visit her til the paparazzi fervour dies down.

I am on the phone when I reach her apartment lobby and about to enter pass security.

"Yes Ellie, don't worry, I am just getting in."

"Excuse me", I hear someone say loudly and I turn to see it is a man with a photographer's camera.

"Yes?"

"I couldn't help but overhear that you were talking to someone named Ellie. You weren't talking to Eleanor James by any chance?"

By the sound of her name being said, countless other photographers start to gather around me and they quickly start to ask questions.

"What is Eleanor doing now?" "How serious is she about James Evans?" "Is she in love?" "Is she going to marry James?" "Has she already married James?" "Why is she hiding, is she pregnant?" "Are you her friend?" "What do you think about them dating, do you think it will last?" "Have they broken up?" "Is she dating someone else?"

On and on the questions went and I stood there dazed, frozen on the spot and unsure of what to do. The man who had first addressed me and asked me about Ellie quickly grabs my hand and takes me inside the lobby while the building security guards handle the growing paparazzi outside.

"I am sorry about starting that commotion. I should have spoken softer so that the others had not noticed."

"It's ok", I say still recovering from my brush with paparazzi.

"If you don't mind, I just wanted to know how Eleanor was doing. She is an ambitious young star and very talented. I had interviewed her when she first started and I knew that she would do great in the industry. I recognized you as you were with her that day and she said you were her best friend and moral support. I know that she was very focused on her work and not on dating, so all this press about her love life must be difficult for her?"

I look at the reporter and feel that he is being genuine in his concern. He did, afterall, save me from the mob outside so I tell him that he was right about the situation.

"Ellie is very young -only twenty-three- and wants to focus on her work. Although she admires and likes James a lot, she is not looking for anything serious at the moment. Her schedule over the next few months will make it very hard for her to continue dating. I just wish that the paparazzi would leave her to continue with her acting dreams and not focus so much on her love life."

"Thank you, I understand. Thank you for giving me that statement and if you dont mind, can I use it for an news article?"

"Sure. If it will makes things better for Ellie, then go ahead."

The next morning, the same reporter would print an 'exclusive interview with a close friend of Eleanor James' and repeat what I had stated. Over the next few days and weeks, the paparazzi continue to gather at her apartment footsteps but soon would give up their hunt, seeing that Ellie is not seen dating anyone anymore.

Ellie tells me that after this crazy date debacle, she vows to make her other dates low-key, if and when she goes back to dating. She says that she wants dating to remain as dating and not become a production or a circus.

As a friend, I am grateful that I was there to help. Luckily I made the right choice in trusting the one reporter that was actually concerned for her welfare among the sea of paparazzi.

Chapter Thirty: Como una Hija (Like a daughter)

The paparazzi ferver has finally died down and things become quieter, and thankfully, much calmer for Ellie. I go visit her building, this time without any difficulty or without encountering any boisterous crowd outside, and am greeted warmly by Ellie's maid and helper Rosa at her apartment.

"Ms. Eleanor has gone for a jog and will be back here soon. Please come inside dear and get comfortable, should I get you anything to drink?", asks Rosa kindly.

I decline the drink but accept her invitation and go inside the apartment to wait for Ellie. Ellie's apartment is sleek and modern and decorated with pictures of her, her family and the two of us on every wall. There are pictures that show her travels from around the world, of Ellie in every location, smiling in front of the Eiffel tower or the Taj Mahal, in front of beautiful cherry blossoms in Japan or hiking on top of Mount Kilimanjaro, with a colorful Toucan in the amazon jungle or with a snobby looking Llama in Machu Picchu. There are pictures of Ellie in the sun, of her in the rain, her playing in the sand or her diving into a waterfall.

There is a digital frame on the living room table with even more of Ellie's favorite pictures, us from our awkward teenager years, both in braces, smiling toothily at the camera. Pictures of us together in our co-ordinated Halloween costumes. Pictures of Hammy, her 'handsome' hamster with the bow ties from her childhood. I continue to look at the picture frames and Rosa comes and offers me some snacks to munch on. Rosa is a jolly and warm lady, around my mom's age, hired by Ellie to help her with cooking and cleaning whenever she is in the city.

"You must be Ms. Cassandra? Lovely dark hair and beautiful green eyes...Ms. Eleanor talks about you all the time and I feel like I know you! Ms. Eleanor is such a nice young lady and it hardly feels like I work for her. She is my favorite person to work for and I have *many* employers through the agency that I work for."

I blush at Rosa's compliment but am pleased that she likes Ellie so much. "Do you work for other people too? What are they like?", I ask curious.

"Si! I have other famous young actresses that I get hired temporarily for as well but none are like Ms. Eleanor. I look forward to when Ms. Eleanor comes back from her work and travels, and God Bless her, she specifically asks for me from the agency each time! I tell my familia that Ms. Eleanor treats me like a daughter would. She wakes up early in the morning, while the other actresses don't even get up til noon and you know what she does? She makes me coffee! She has a cup ready for me as soon as I come to work and she makes me sit with her and asks me questions about myself and my family. She even practices Spanish with me nearly every day...she is getting quite good at it too!"

I am not surprised at Ellie's warmth and good nature and I have always been envious of her ability to learn new languages quickly since she was in school. I myself stumble with common spanish phrases despite taking it in high school.

Ellie returns from her jog, still looking immaculate with only a slight flush in her cheeks that give any indication of her exertion and exercise. She gives me a hug and greets Rosa with a smile and they both start having a conversation in Spanish. I look at them quietly while they continue talking and Rosa turns her attention towards me, she laughs and asks me good-naturedly,"Why Ms. Cassandra, why don't you join us too? You can practice your Spanish with us!"

"Thanks Mrs. Rosa...I am afraid that I don't know a lot of Spanish but I do remember the phrase *'Deja que te diga cosas al oído, para que te acuerdes si no estás conmigo'*. I just don't remember exactly what it means."

Both Ellie and Rosa laugh. "Who have you been telling that to Cassie? You do know that it means 'Let me tell you things in your ear so you will remember if you're not with me'. Am I correct Rosa?"

Rosa smiles brightly, "Yes dear, that is the right translation. Well done!"

I don't think that I could have turned a deeper shade of red than after hearing Ellie's english translation of the phrase I had said so casually. Rosa saves me from my embarassment and says that it was good practice for the future when I do have someone to whisper in the ear to and that she was impressed with my clear pronounciation of the spanish words.

Ellie would continue to tease me about this for a while, saying that she wanted to meet my *novio secreto.* I would eventually find the humor in the situation and say that I wanted to meet him too.

AISHA UROOJ

*secret boyfriend

∞ ∞ ∞

Chapter Thirty-One: Where Monsters are Real

When I was growing up, I was terrified of monsters. I thought that they hid in the dark corners of the house and lurked outside during the night. As a kid, I imagined sharp nails and monstrous teeth. When I grew up, I knew that monsters were real and that they could be anywhere...and that they looked just like you and me.

For months, Ellie has been on edge and I finally know why. Mrs. James calls me suddenly one day and tells me that Ellie had an accident and was in the hospital.

Elllie has been hurt by a stalker, one who had been stalking her for months. First it started with letters, then phone calls and random visits to her apartment. Each time security intervened and set the intruder on his way. Ellie didn't press charges thinking that he will give up eventually and find another source of entertainment.

His harmless hobby was more than a passing liking however, it soon turned to dangerous obsession. In his attempt to make Ellie his own, the stalker brazenly tries to kidnap her midday while she was out on her afternoon jog. He drags her through the streets and onlookers jump to her rescue hearing her scream. He pulls out a knife and puts it on Ellie's throat, screaming that if he can't have her then she should die with him. That is the moment when the security guard opens fire, killing Ellie's stalker.

It was Mrs. James that tells me all that had happened with Ellie in the last few months when I reach the hospital. I am a little hurt that Ellie didn't tell me what had been going on nor that she called me after the ordeal and when she was ok.

I rush to Ellie's bedside to comfort her and give her a hug. Looking at her bandages and bruises, however, I start to cry instead. Ellie becomes distressed seeing me cry.

"This is why I didn't want to tell you...I rather bear all my injuries and more than to see you cry Cassie!"

I am shocked, not by her words but by something else...this moment felt familiar to me. Someone else has told me the exact thing that Ellie had just said, lying on a hospital bed as well. He also had been close to my heart once.

I try my best to quickly stop my tears and as I wipe my eyes on my sleeve, Ellie passes me a tissue.

"You are too much...you know that Cassie. I love you, you crybaby!"

"Thanks Ellie", I say sniffling. "I am a total wuss, I know... I will try to be brave like you. I love you too!"

Chapter Thirty-Two: Tears for pain, Tears for Joy

The last time I had been in the hospital was when John had gotten into an accident during our date. We went on a bike ride for our second date, roaming around the pretty spots in our neighborhood. John was having a lot of fun and he was excitedly showing me the locations where he had looked for me when we had first met and I had disappeared on him.

"Where did you go that day Cassie? I can't figure it out! I looked for you everywhere."

"I might have gone to the library, usually I go there..."

"No it can't have been there, it was the first spot that I checked!"

"I know a shortcut through the park, maybe I went through that?"

"I know that spot! I checked every spot and covered all the

grounds Cassie but you simply vanished. You don't have Harry's invisibility cloak by any chance?", asks John referring to Harry Potter.

"No but I wish I did! It would be a nice change from running away from people", I say laughing.

"Did the earth swallow you or did you hide in the clouds? That is the only way I couldn't have found you", teases John.

"Well...you might be close. There is a tree house that I go to but very rarely."

"So you weren't on ground but up on a tree? No wonder why I couldn't find you!"

John gets very excited about his discovery but in his excitement he doesn't pay attention to the incoming car. The driver of the car is distracted as well and he nearly collides directly with John. I scream as the car narrowly drives into John, he swerves in time but John rides onto the pavement and collides with a pole. I rush next to him as he laid sprawled on the pavement with one of his arm rotated in a weird angle.

"Oh my God John! Are you alright?!"

"I am ok Cassie...but I think that my arm might be fractured."

The distracted driver gets out of his car and rushes towards John to see how he was, seeing his condition, he quickly calls for an ambulance. I stay next to John in the ambulance, all the way to the hospital. His x-ray showed that he had a broken arm and soon he was put in a cast.

As he layed on the hospital bed, I see him wince uncomfortably and after seeing him in pain, I start to cry.

"Please don't cry Cassie, I am ok."

"But you broke a arm...it must be hurting," I say crying.

"It is not that bad actually..."

"He could have really hurt you...my heart nearly stopped when you were hit by the pole."

"That was a little inconvenient but it could have been worse.."

At his words, I start crying even more. John gets visibly upset seeing me cry, he tries to console me but I don't stop the tear-works.

"Cassie...please don't.....I would rather break another arm than to see you cry!"

I don't stop crying.

"Fine...I will add another leg."

I still have tears in my eyes but I am shocked at his statement, "That is a bit much John...breaking two arms and a leg over my tears!"

"It is not even close...I will rather break all the bones in my body than see you cry. I will gladly accept my life as a rubber man."

I laugh at the ridiculousness of his statement. I don't know how or when it happened but I was holding John's hand. We had never held hands til that point, it feels warm and I feel safe with him. John continues talking about all the things he would do to stop me from crying and some of his ideas are so outrageous that by the end, I had tears streaming down my face from laughing so much.

Chapter Thirty-Three: Demons from the Past

The doctor warns us that Ellie might suffer from post-traumatic stress disorder after the stalker event and that we should keep an eye out for any signs of changes to her thoughts, emotions, or behavior. Mrs. James, however, seemed also worried about something else. She worries that it might trigger another old memory in her daughter.

"I hope that Eleanor is not reminded of the time she was abducted by this horrible event..."

"Ellie was abducted?! She...never told me about that."

"It was before she met you dear and she hardly remembers it herself."

"Mrs. James...if you don't mind telling me, what had happened?"

"Eleanor had been kidnapped on her way to school. She had been for three days before we were able to arrange for the kidnappers the ransom that they had demanded at the location that they wanted. I wish it hadn't been three days..."

"That is terrible! Ellie must have been so frightened! I can't imagine being a little kid and being kidnapped for three days. She must have felt so alone."

"Yes dear...as a mother you can't imagine what I went through...it was like my breath had been snatched away from me! I could only breathe after she returned."

"I am so sorry Mrs. James...I should have thought about my words before I spoke them. I didn't mean to hurt you."

"It's ok dear....I know how you feel. I had felt the same during the endless dark days Ellie had been taken away."

"What happened after she returned?"

"Surprisingly, not much...Eleanor had seem mostly unaffected after she returned except for getting a few nightmares. Her therapist had said perhaps she had repressed her memory of the event in order to cope with it...and that another such event might make her remember it again."

"Oh my poor Ellie....she had to go through such a thing again. Do you think that we should talk to her about it?"

"No dear, I think it will be better if Eleanor brings it up herself. I don't want to remind her in case she has forgotten. It is best not to trigger any uncomfortable or painful memories at a time like this."

I look at Ellie, through the hospital's door window, worried but she seems to be alright. She is laughing and happily talking to her dad, eating from a bag of chips.

She told me that since she was at the hospital, that gave her a reason to get a break from her training and from her diet for a couple of hours. Ellie refused to see a therapist after her stay at the hospital reassuring us that she was fine.

Mrs. James confided to me her thoughts and said that perhaps Ellie's busy schedule would keep her sufficiently occupied and distracted from ever thinking about the dark days from her past.

For Ellie's sake, I hope for the same as well... I pray that no dark thoughts ever reach the surface or see the light of day. I pray that any hidden demons that could haunt Ellie lay dormant forever.

Chapter Thirty-Four: Alien Musical

Ellie wounds soon healed and life returned to the way it was before. Any painful memory was soon forgotten as Ellie continued pouring her heart and soul into her work.

Ellie soon stars in a musical production which she help co-write as well. The comedy musical production 'Alien MacMaelien' is wildly successful, being hailed as a modern-day Midsummer's Night Dream.

The musical is about MacMaelian, an alien outcast who finds massive success on Earth as a rock star. Based on his success and popularity, the world leaders want him to be Earth's ambassador to his home planet and to invite his leader to an intergalactic diplomatic meeting. What the people of Earth don't know is that MacMaelian is an exile, who had lied about his extravagant life and rank on his home planet and had been dumped here unceremoniously on a shooting star.

Back on his planet, MacMaelian had wooed his leader's daughter, as well as secretly his son, through his massive charm and charisma (and a love potion) in order to rise up the ranks. When his engagement to the leader's daughter is announced, his betrayal to the son also becomes apparent.

Instead of ordering execution for MacMaelian, the two siblings become engulfed in a civil war with each other over MacMaelian that threatens to tear the kingdom apart. To save his planet, the leader orders the secret exile of MacMaelian and disguises his disappearance as an act of cowardice and fleeing. Now Mac-Maelian is faced with a challenge, either to reveal his truth to the people on Earth and face another exile when his true deceptive nature is revealed or contact his home planet and risk the alien civil war spilling over here. He faces the greatest challenge of his life and in the musical he tries desperately to save the one person who is dearest to him on any planet: Himself.

"Ellie, I don't know whether to laugh at MacMaelian or have pity on him?"

"Yeah, he is a polarizing character. I can't believe some people love him so much."

"His character is outrageous. He uses anything to make people love him: poetry, flattery, bribe, potions, hypnosis, brownies. The musical is amazing overall..what a great backstory!"

"I thought that the musical writer must have been hallucinating when he wrote it. It is so bizarre at times..."

"No, no Ellie, it is so funny! Didn't you help co-write it too?"

"I had a few ideas for MacMaelien and he went with it. I think he gave me too much credit though. He might have done it to get more publicity by having me as a co-writer..."

"Ellie I think that you are too modest. You have always had a flair for ingenuity and creativity! You could be a writer for sure!"

"Says Ms. Major in English Literature...if anyone could be the writer, it will be you Cassie.."

I blush at her comment. "Ellie, I need to graduate first of all before I can do anything. I still have finals to deal with!"

"How is your favorite Professor by the way? Does he still have the same sense of humor?"

"Professor K? Yes! He would probably say that "MacMaelien puts the Mack in alien"...or something similar."

"Ha ha that is terrible! Almost as bad as MacMaelien though..."

"How did you come up with the idea of such a character Ellie? He really seems out of this world."

"Actually he was inspired by your blind date with Mr. Confident Entrepreneur.."

"Ha ha...Oh God no wonder MacMaelien seemed so familiar to me!"

"Yeah Cassie, you should go on more blind dates like that."

"No way! Not for all the successful musicals in the world!!"

Ellie laughs at my protest. The musical continues with its massive success and is translated and produced in several languages around the world.

It seemed characters like MacMaelien (and Mr. Entrepreneur) are universally identifiable and universally comical in every corner of the world. I often wondered if my blind date had seen the musical and bragged about being the inspiration behind Ellie's genius work.

At least this time, out of all his tall claims, this would be partially true.

Chapter Thirty-Five: Ellie's Big Birthday Bash

June have arrived and that means that Ellie's birthday will be here soon. Every year her parents throw a big birthday celebration in her honor, each time a more luxurious and fancier affair than the year before.

Some years it has been in exotic locations like Hawaii or Cancun and in preparation, I would have to dive deep into my closet to bring out my only luggage case, still brand new as it has barely been used by me.

I would miss Buddy alot during the days away and would have to tearfully leave him behind with my parents. This year, thankfully, the birthday bash is set at the most exclusive private club in town. I receive a phone call from Ellie and she doesn't sound very excited about the planned festivities.

"Hi Cassie", she says missing her usual energy.

"Ellie, is everything alright? You don't sound like your normal self."

"No I am alright. Just wanted to confirm the location of the birthday bash with you."

I am not convinced. "Aren't you excited Ellie?"

"I don't know Cassie, we have a big celebration every year and my parents go over the top with everything. I was thinking, maybe it can be low key this time?"

"Ellie, I am sure that they will understand if you don't want to do it big this year."

"I am not sure they will...in any case, I don't want to disappoint my parents as they have already paid for everything."

"Is something wrong Ellie? I thought you liked all the commotion and chaos. Are you turning into me by any chance? I am not sure the world can handle two of my kind."

Ellie laughs. "No Cassie...it is just sometimes it all feels a bit much. Do you know what I mean?"

"You mean that instead of four chocolate fountains, three cakes and fireworks, you only want two chocolate fountains, one cake and firecrackers?"

"No I didn't mean that...", she pauses to think. "The food is usually awesome..."

"What about the hors-d'oeuvre?...they have calamari, your favorite."

"Dammit Cassie, you are making me hungry!"

"Ellie I am drooling myself over here. You know that your birthday is the one day that I am not on a diet!"

"....as oppose to any other day of the year?", teases Ellie. She seems to be in a better mood now. "You know what Cassie, let it be a big one this year. It is not like I will turn twenty-four twice!"

"Yes! That is more like it, let's celebrate your big day... woohoo for being twenty-four!"

Ellie laughs. I am happy to hear her sounding like her normal self and to know that she cheered up. We spend the remaining conversation deciding on what we would wear for the party.

The birthday venue looked like it was decorated for a wedding. There were beautiful white rose and white lilies bouquets at every table, along with champagne bottles and Swarovski crystal swan figurines placed as gifts on the table for each guest.

The theme for the birthday party this year was an ice palace and Ellie was dressed fitted for an ice princess, in her high neck long sleeve white mermaid gown with intricate bodice. She got me a beautiful sheer silver crewneck gown with crystal embellishments to wear on her birthday, a favor from her designer friend.

Ellie's birthday cake is three tiered and in the shape of a giant snowflake. There are ice sculptures everywhere, crystal chandeliers and icicles hanging from the ceiling and a beautiful ice dragon fountain centrepiece that poured out drinks for the guests to enjoy. There is even a small orchestra playing Baroque music throughout the night, making the atmosphere feel more magical and wonderful.

Her parents unveiled her birthday present in front of the guests, a brand new white Lamborghini tied with a huge silver and white bow on the top. They certainly didn't spare any expense on their daughter's birthday but Ellie was grateful for their presence and love, above all things.

As always, the party ends with a spectacular display of fireworks and we all toast together for Ellie's good health and happiness.

Chapter Thirty-Six: What Money Can't Buy

W hat do you get a person who has everything? Each year for her birthday, I face the daunting task of buying Ellie a present that she doesn't already own.

This year Ellie's parents bought her a Lamborghini for her twenty-fourth birthday, so me giving her a luxury car is out of the question. Well...it was a far stretch to begin with, looking at the paltry figure in my bank savings, but I still like to think that it could have been an option.

Next, she already has haute couture designers clamoring for her attention and for her to try on their beautiful one-of-a-kind original creations customized to her body and fit, so I can't compete there and besides, I already found her a great vintage dress two years ago.

Ellie is the spokesperson for a major cosmetic brand along with being the face of an illustrious French fashion house and now has her very own makeup team, so she hardly needs yet another cosmetic gift set. Not only her sponsors, but also her many fans send her countless presents through the mail and her more avid admirers and suitors, shower her with expensive jewellery.

Although she always appreciate what I give her, like for instance the friendship bracelet I made her in high school and which Ellie wore for months til the threads wore out. She still has it and keeps it in her jewellery box! No, as her best friend, I consider it a sacred duty to get her a present truly worthy of our friendship. I try asking her for hints as to what she would like but it proves to be an fruitless endeavor and doesn't provide me any more clarification either.

"Ellie, is there anything you would like for your birthday?"

"We could have a girl's day out?"

"We are already doing that. No, I meant as your present. What do you want?"

"Whatever you had in mind."

"A Gourmet Food of the Month Club membership?"

"Wait...don't ruin the surprise Cassie. Don't tell me what you are getting me!"

"Ellie, you always lavish me with great gifts...I am just looking for a clue to getting something you really want! Help me out here..."

"I mean it Cassie...whatever you have in mind. You always put great thought into your gifts. Remember how you gave me one of the pearl strand from the Tahitian pearl necklace you got...the heirloom from your grandma? You said that she had two granddaughters and not just one. What could be more thoughtful than that?"

"But it's true Cassie, she loved you too so that was the right thing to do."

"I am sure I will love anything you give me."

"Anything? What if I gave you the dancing hamster again?"

"I would love that!! You were the one who got crazy when I played it so many times.."

"Oh God...How did I forget?! The annoying tune was stuck in my head for months...ok, maybe not the hamster again. I don't want to repeat a gift anyway. Come on Ellie, give me some hint.."

"Ok if you insist, get me something that money can't buy."

"Something that money can't buy?"

"Yes! You have your hint now."

Ellie's clue left me perplexed. What could I get her that money can't buy? Love, Health, Happiness all came to mind...but how to give them? One can't exactly bottle them and hand them out...or could I?

I thought about Ellie's apartment and all the pictures that she had displayed throughout her walls. Those pictures made her very happy. She had pictures everywhere except the kitchen fridge. Maybe I can get her customized photo fridge magnets? It was a good idea except she already has all the pictures that I would have of us together, so I needed pictures that she won't have. I decide to give her a picture of me with Buddy, but this time Buddy will be wearing a bowtie, in homage to her child-hood pet hamster Hammy.

Buddy makes it very hard for me to take this picture since he does not like wearing the bowtie, a déjà vu situation of Hammy hiding in the slippers also because of his bowtie.

I hire a student photographer who lived in the same apartment building as me to help take the photos. I even had the bright idea of taking the picture outdoors in a park in order to get good lighting. At first the photo session goes well as Buddy is co-oper-ating despite his obvious discomfort with the bowtie. The stu-dent photographer manages to get a few solo pictures of Buddy.

Next, he wants Buddy and me to pose together...this is when it all turns to chaos.

"Buddy come back here, stop chasing that squirrel!"

"Buddy, don't chew the bowtie...we need it in the picture. It's for Ellie!"

"Buddy that was just a car horn, no need to hide behind the tree!"

"Buddy, where are you going?...no, that wasn't Ellie! Come back here!"

"Oh for Heaven's sake! Why did that squirrel come back again?!"

Twenty-seven attempts later, we finally manage to have three unblurry pictures in total, one of Buddy alone and two with me. It was by the last picture that Buddy finally comes sits next to me quietly.

Perhaps that squirrel had finally gone away or perhaps Buddy had pity on my most pitiable and pathetic state, an aftermath of all of the sweating and huffing chasing after him. I thank the student photographer for his time and although I only have three usable pictures, I feel bad to bother him for more. I had to decide now, out of the three photos, which ones should I use?

Buddy looks great in the solo picture with thankfully his bowtie still intact. One of his picture with me is good enough, but the third one is a total mess. In this picture, Buddy's bowtie is in his mouth, barely hanging on and I am sitting beside him sweaty and muddy, laughing like a mad woman, most likely experiencing a case of hysteria after the squirrel trauma.

What do I do? I can't just give Ellie two pictures so I decide, reluctantly, to include all three.

Ellie loved my gift! So much in fact that she had tears of joy and couldn't stop gushing over the photos. She immediately puts the photo magnets on the fridge.

Her favorite picture out of all the three is the last one, which she calls 'perfect snapshot of real love (and squirrel chaos)'. She liked it so much in fact that she has a smaller version printed and carries it with her in her purse always.

I smile as I managed to find her something that she had wanted. Hearing her laughter and seeing her happiness after she opened my present was her accidental yet priceless gift returned to me, it was a feeling that no money could have bought.

Chapter Thirty-Seven: Life Exams

I haven't heard from Ellie in a while but I have been too busy studying for my finals to call her back. It is the final stretch and I would finally earn my undergraduate degree in English Lit.

I am trying to fulfill my promise to my parents as Ellie already did to hers by reaching her goals and becoming a superstar. I wonder about what I would do after getting my undergrad. I think hard but I don't have any epiphanies jump at me so, just like always, I push the thought aside for the future. I really do need to stop procrastinating about it. Perhaps what I really need is a divine intervention, a sign, a clue, a dream to point me in the right direction?

My weeks are spend furiously cramming for my exams. I only occasionally get a text from Ellie. She knows my deadlines, perhaps she is giving me space to be studious Cassie?

I walk around in a zombie state with my textbook atow, often forgetting to eat or drink. It is only when Buddy barks furiously for his breakfast, then lunch and then dinner that I remember to eat something at those times as well.

All the missed sleep and lost hours with Ellie come to a climatic end on results day. I pass with honors! I am free! I have officially conquered one element of adulthood and can now spend time celebrating with the best people in the whole wide world: My best human friend and my best furry friend.

I call Ellie with the good news. Her voice sounds muffled, like she has a cold.

"Ellie, I did it! I passed! We should celebrate together!"

"Cassie that is fantastic! You have an undergrad in English Lit now, that is amazing. We should definitely do a get-together!" She starts to cough.

"Oh no Ellie, are you sick? I will come over. Don't worry about celebrating right now, we can do it later."

"Yes Cassie, I might have something. I don't want you to catch it too and you still have to attend graduation. Let's meet up at graduation day? My cold would have cleared up by then."

"But you never get sick. I hope that you are not overworking yourself. You should give yourself time to rest. Ok we can meet on graduation day....Eeee! I can't believe I am going to graduate!"

"Ok awesome Cassie, we will have fun on your big day!"

Although I am bummed that I don't get to see Ellie til graduation day, she really did sound like she had a bad cold. I want to visit her but she made me promised that I wouldn't til she was better.

My big day arrives and I don't see Ellie anywhere in the convocation hall. My parents see me onstage and they wave at me from the audience. I smile and happily wave back to them. My eyes continue to search for Ellie.

Where was she? Perhaps she got delayed at a film shooting? I wait nervously in line with the other graduates-to-be. As it is a small private university, a big star like Ellie wouldn't have to worry about security here. I do worry however that Ellie might miss my big moment. I can't look for her anymore as I hear my name being called!

"Cassandra Leonora Grace. English Literature with Honors."

As I receive my scroll, I hear the audience clap politely but one voice rises out of the crowd. "Yay Cassie! Way to go!"

It is Ellie! I see her in the audience with a bouquet of flowers and the biggest teddy bear that I have ever seen in my life! Ellie is almost hidden behind its monstrous size! I laugh in glee as it is so good to see Ellie here. She didn't miss my big day! She later would say that she wouldn't have missed it for the world. As I couldn't carry the enormous teddy around, I leave it at home with Buddy, telling him that it was a gift from Ellie and warned him that he shouldn't even think about destroying it unless he wanted her to be angry at him.

After the ceremony, Ellie, my parents and I would spend some time together at a chinese restuarant talking and it feels like we are transported back to high school days again.

Ellie says that she had missed quiet moments like these. When we both arrive at my apartment after the dinner, we find that Buddy is missing and nowhere to be seen. After searching throughout the apartment, we finally locate Buddy in a corner along with the missing graduation present. Both Ellie and I would laugh at the sight of Buddy snoring on top of the giant teddy.

Chapter Thirty-Eight: Of Beast and Sleeping Beauty

The weather around here has been all thunderstorms lately and the city hasn't seen the sun shine in many days. I don't like it when the weather gets gloomy like this as it gives me an ominous and uneasy feeling. I miss seeing the clear blue sky outside my window.

I try to push away my discomfort and Buddy comes snuggling next to me, trying to make me feel better. I stroke his fur and doing so seems to calm me down. Buddy drops something by my feet and I pick it up to see that it is a small figurine of the Beast. 'Where did Buddy find this?', I wonder looking at Beast's figure. I reminisce back to when John took me to see Beauty and the Beast together.

When John had asked me if I wanted to see a movie with him on our first date, I had panicked. He felt like a stranger to me and I had been nervous of the idea of being with him in the dark. I could barely even speak to him because of my shyness.

By the time he asked me to a movie again, I agreed to go with him. After our other dates and time spend together, I felt more safe with him than with any other person I knew. John said that he really wanted to watch one movie out of all the other movies that were playing. He wanted to see Beauty and the Beast together because, according to him, Belle reminded him of me and so he thought that he would like the movie. I remember that I had blushed at his compliment and as always had been touched by his openness and candor.

After the film ends, I ask him what he thought was the best part of the movie and he says,"It was when Belle falls in love with the Beast and lifts his curse. I liked seeing the transformation of Beast into a man after Belle accepts his love."

He then asks me the same question, about what I thought was the best part and I say, "It was when the Beast promises that he would wait for Belle forever, even when he didn't know if she would come back for him."

I look closer at the little figurine in my hand and Beast's expression looks sad, had Belle left him at this point and he had vowed to wait for her forever?

'Of course Beast would wait for Belle', I say wistfully, 'She meant everything to him'.

I think about Beast and his cursed love and I identify with his character more than I ever did before, I understand his sorrow and his longing for Belle and why he would wait for her. I sigh and my heart feels heavy.

I think about what John had said and I say, "No John, I am not like Belle. I was never like Belle. I am cursed too, cursed to wait, just like the Beast."

∞∞∞

The weather doesn't get better. It alternates between rain and fog and as I look from my window, the people moving outside are turned into ghosts and shadows in the mist. The image makes me shiver.

I have a hard time shaking this uneasy feeling away. I think about calling Ellie and I pick up the phone, I call her a few times but she is not answering her phone. Where was she? Why wasn't she picking up the phone? I wish she did, I really want to hear her voice.

Soon after I receive a phone call from Ellie's parents. Maybe they can tell me where Ellie was? I pick up the phone and hear Mrs. James crying on the other end.

"Cassie...our baby is gone. Eleanor is dead."

I stop breathing. "The police came to us in the morning. They said that the maid had found Eleanor passed away in her sleep. We have been asked to come to the morgue to identify her body."

The words "Eleanor" "morgue" "body" scream at me. My mind is in a deeper fog than the one outside my window and I have trouble understanding any of Mrs. James' words. What was she saying? She can't be talking about my Ellie? Ellie can't die...

This time Mr. James is speaking, "Cassie dear, can you please come to the hospital? We can't do this alone, we need you here."

My legs finally start to move towards my apartment door. In my semi-conscious state, I somehow arrive to where Ellie's parents were waiting for me and we are taken to Ellie's 'body'. It is hard for me to believe that she is dead and not simply sleeping. Her golden hair caress her face and her eyes are closed. She can't be dead. I touch her face to wake her from her slumber.

She is cold. My Ellie, who is always warmth herself is freezing to the touch. A sob escapes my lips. I see Mrs. James collapse to the ground and Mr. James hold her hand in tears and agony.

Ellie didn't respond to our cries.

She doesn't move at all. There she laid frozen, unaware of the world around her, far away from any sorrow, deep in her slumber like a sleeping beauty.

∞∞∞

'Accidental overdose' are what the doctors are calling it.

I never thought Ellie would be a victim of an overdose. A girl that brought life into my world be taken away so suddenly. One who brought light and chased away my dark clouds be consumed by darkness herself. Her love, her light succumbed to drugs.

I knew she would sometimes take drugs when she first started in the acting industry, mostly recreational, during the parties and more to be social than anything serious. I had never agreed to it and I would tell her to stop taking it so lightly. She had pretended or had lied to me that she never even looked at them anymore.

How could she do this? How could she be so reckless? She should have known about the danger! She should have known better! Had the trauma after her last incident had her looking for something stronger? Had she be taking more and more to get some relief, til she couldn't anymore? Or was it accidental and a one time thing? Why did she take it when she had so much to live for? Did she think that she was in control when in fact the drugs ended up controlling her?

There is no relief for me in asking these questions when you are not here to answer them. Ellie, why did you face it all alone? Why didn't you tell me?

I will never know about the inner demons that you had been fighting. You didn't tell me.

I wish I had known. I wish I had stopped her death.

All I could do now is wish. I wish she had thought about what could happen. I wish she had sought help before it was too late, before it consumed her and her life and left us broken. I think about her parents and I wonder if they regret agreeing to her acting career. I wonder if they regret saying yes to her leaving high school. I wonder that if they had known about the outcome, would they have locked Ellie away forever to protect her?

I would have.

They grieve that as parents they have to bury their child. They grieve at the loss of their baby, their daughter, their angel and I can't say or do anything that can bring her back to us.

Chapter Thirty-Nine: A Lost Friend

During university, I had sometimes considered writing as a possible future option and when I thought about it more, I had wanted the subject to be on friendship.

I would scribble bits and ideas on to paper, hoping to eventually surprise Ellie with a completed work. Ellie had been healthy and alive then. I didn't know that I would complete this work but as her in my memory...an ode to our friendship.

Dead at twenty-four.

It didn't make sense. The number didn't make sense. Her death didn't make sense. None of it made sense.

As I was chosen to read the eulogy at her funeral, countless people came to me remarking how my thoughts had captured her spirit as she had lived. My thought gave words to the tremendous grief and indescribable loss they felt.

Ellie had touched so many lives in her short stay on earth, both on the screen and in person. She had amassed a huge following, it seemed impossible, but even more than when she was alive, almost a cult like public obsession.

The words "young movie legend" were being thrown around as she won accolade after accolade posthumously. I looked at the gathered crowd in the church and saw some familiar faces like Mr. Chris, Ms. Carla, Mrs. Rosa, sitting teary-eyed and grief-stricken with her family, but most of the faces are unknown to me and I wonder in what way had Ellie touched their lives. Her eulogy is printed in countless newspaper and shared online as people saw it echo the sentiments in their hearts and mind. It seemed like, as I did, the whole world was grieving the loss of a friend.

We all found our ways to mourn and come to terms with her passing. Ellie's parents opened a rehabilitation and treatment centre for drug addiction in her name. Ellie's parents also contributed funds to PTSD and late-onset PTSD research, the latter was most likely what had driven Ellie to addiction.

They would also go from one high school to another across the country to share their story with the students. They talked of their grief to the young students in hopes that it would prevent them from making the same mistake that Ellie made and to make them realize the perils of addiction. They would plea to anyone listening to not let anyone suffer alone in silence and if they weren't sure where or how to start, to not to be afraid to seek help. Most of all they didn't want another family going through what they were going through, losing a child to addiction.

I also found a way to mourn her death and for hours on end, I would write my thoughts onto paper. Hours turned into days and days turned into weeks. As I wrote about her, words became my anchor and writing became the lifeline. I was finally to be something, a writer.

My soul would take flight on paper, just like Ellie's had going city to city for her acting aspirations. Just like her's had in every role she played on camera. Just like her's would still have performing, if only she hadn't given in to addiction. I close my eyes, too tired to think anymore.

Buddy misses Ellie terribly too. His ears and tail remains drooped. Early morning before our walks, he would scratch his paws on the front door, whimper sadly and wait for his missing favorite visitor. He howls hauntingly when he sees Ellie's picture on the news or when her movie plays on TV. I hug him tight and tell him that I missed her too. We both loved her the same way and we share our grief together.

A few weeks after Ellie's death, I received a copy of the will from the estate attorney as I was listed as one of the beneficiaries, included with the document was also a hand-written letter by Ellie. The letter is dated from a year ago, my hands trembled as I start to read, tears well in my eyes as I hear Ellie's voice once again through the words on her letter.

Dear Cassie,

If you are reading this letter, it is probably after you heard the bad news of me being dead.

Don't worry, I didn't have a premonition nor had I contemplated dying suddenly, I would have told you about that, but after my accident my lawyer advised me to think about drafting a will. I am sure you got the legal documents in all the legal fine print glory...I just wanted to pen you an handwritten letter that would give a more proper adieu.

If you are reading this letter at age hundred and one, then congratulations to you (and hopefully me as well) for living to be a century old! The sum that I have left for you, you can will to your most capable, or favorite, child or grandchild or great grandchild (unfair favoritism is allowed in very old grannies).

However, if you have truly become an cranky old toad, and are not in a sharing mood or feel anyone is worthy enough, than you can feel free to finally buy that donut shop and indulge in all the sugary treats that your heart desires. Trust me, as I am already dead, I won't be haunting you for your diet anymore. Similarly, you can also feel free to donate it to any charity of your choice or do as you please with the money.

If you are reading this letter much sooner than at an old age, then my dear Cassie, I am sorry for the grief that you are feeling because of my death. Although it might hurt you to read this, but in a way I am glad that I passed away before you because I don't think I could have beared the same sorrow.

Cassie I want you to use this fund to fulfill your life's dream. If you have finally decided to accept your gift of being a deep and sensitive soul and became a writer, it would bring much joy to my deceased self if you used my insignificant money to publish your first novel.

You might protest that the sum is not insignificant at all however the money is no use to me dead and I would rather find some peace in the thought that my best friend used it for a meaningful purpose. I know you feel indecisive but deep down I know you have finally chosen what you want to do. Trust in yourself Ellie and trust me when I say that you are destined for great things. You should share your thoughts with the world as the world would be much better for it.

I will make you a promise Cassie, I will put my untimely departure to good use. How you may ask? I will talk to the Big Guy and ask him to send you back the love of your life (you know how good I am with negotiations!). Even though you don't say his name, I know that you often think about him.... and despite you giving your best efforts at dating and love, your heart has not belonged to anyone since him.

You deserve everything my dear friend. I am just sorry that I can't wrap my arms around you to say I love you. But I love you Cassie.

Don't grieve my death, my dear friend, for Life comes with both thorns and roses.

Forever Yours,

Ellie

p.s. Please give my hug to Buddy if he is around and missing me. I love you too Buddy

Just when I thought that I had run out of tears, Ellie's letter brings me to the breaking point. Life was so unfair, she didn't want to die so young...I had lost my friend, I had lost my world.

Chapter Forty: Promised Return

A year passes by like a blur, it was around this time that John found me, likely as a gift send from Ellie looking out for me from the heavens above.

My first published writing had brought me out of obscurity and into the sight of my first love. I receive a phone call from a person named John Damon, who had been looking for a Cassandra Grace. We agree to meet in person and I come face to face with the person who I had often thought about over the years.

I see him and I wonder if I should I let myself believe that he had thought about me too? John is not the teenage boy that I had known in high school but now he stood in front of me as a 26-year old man, grown more sombre and handsome with the passage of time.

"How are you Cassandra?", asks an older John

"I am......not alright", I finally admit to another person and I am surprised at my own frank admission to him.

"What can I do to make you feel better?", he says concerned. His amber eyes as lovely as yesteryear.

"Can you.... forgive me?"

"Forgive you?"

"Yes, I know that I don't deserve it but can you forgive me John? I am sorry for how I treated you."

"You don't have anything to apologize for."

"Yes, I do. You have always been sweet, kind, understanding to me....and I acted cold in return. I have felt guilty ever since."

"You shouldn't have felt guilty, it was a long time ago."

"I do feel terribly guilty! I was young and didn't know any better but that is no excuse. I shouldn't have done it."

"It is ok."

"Are you sure?", I ask looking at him.

"Yes....I am glad that you did."

I wasn't expecting to hear this from him, I am genuinely surprised. "You are....glad?"

"Yes, you heard it correctly. I am glad."

"Why would you be glad? John I ignored you. I wouldn't answer back to your messages. I wouldn't pick up your calls. You tried to reach me several times but each time I wouldn't even give you a chance to say anything...I was horrible to you..."

He answers, "I know you did that because you were hurting and that my moving away was hard for you as much it was for me. Honestly, if you had remained sweet to me, my dear Cassie, I would have fallen even more in love with you than I already was, it would have made it impossible for me to leave you. We were only teenagers then with the whole world before us, perhaps we needed the time apart from each other to grow and then to find each other again once more."

I remain speechless and he continues,"I won't lie Cassie, I have often thought about you and wondered where you were and what you were doing. If you would like, I want us to get to know each other again."

There it was...I had heard from him what I wanted to believe all these years. He had finally said that he had been in love with me back then.

I look at him, loss for words and he reaches for my hands. He kisses the fingertips gently and my body warms at his touch. I cup his face gently into my hands and he closes his eyes slowly, as if he were waiting for my touch. Oh how I had missed him! He had remembered me. He told me that he had often thought about me.

We would continue to see each other a few times each week. John is as patient and loving as long before, when he asks where I had wanted to go with him on our dates, I had said to simply just go for walks together.

He obliges my request and we would walk and talk during our hikes, often with Buddy accompanying us happily. We would share our life stories from the days after high school and to just before we met again. We walk near a pond and I see a swan paddle through the reflected autumn colors in the water.

"Cassie, I use to wander around town looking for you on my bike. I had hoped to find you around every corner that I turned. I really wanted to bump into you again."

"With your bike?", I ask hesitantly.

"Well...it didn't work the first time..."

We both laugh at the memory of our first meeting when he had literally bumped into me with his bike.

After seeing me laugh, John looks at me and says, "I had missed hearing your laughter Cassie."

"I think I had forgotten how to... after Ellie died."

"That must have been hard for you. I am sorry."

"I am the one who is sorry...it is all my fault John, I should have saved Ellie."

"It is not your fault Cassie."

"I should have known, I should have helped her."

"She hid it from everyone Cassie, no one could have known."

"I failed her as her friend. I will never forgive myself."

"Don't say that... Ellie would be sad to see you like this. She loved you."

"I wish I had told her how much I loved her. I should have told her that every day, she should have never felt all alone. I can't anymore, now she is gone."

"I am sure she knew Cassie. You can't predict what is going to happen in life, none of us can. We can just try to appreciate life while we have it."

"You are right John. My biggest regret is not telling her that I loved her every day. I don't want to make that mistake ever again", I say with tears in my eyes. "John I wanted to tell you...."

"...I know what you want to tell me."

"You do?"

"Yes...I want to say it to you as well. I had lost the chance to tell you many years ago and I had agonized over if I would get another chance in this life. I truly cannot wait another second to tell you this. I love you Cassandra Grace, I always have and when we met again, I knew that I always will. I love you so much Cassie."

John kisses me deeply after declaring his love. This time I kiss him back with tears streaming down my face.

"I love you John. I love you with all my heart. I wanted to tell you that and I promise that I will every day."

He holds my hand and I rest my head on his shoulders. I think about how fate had brought us back together. I think about all the uncertainty we faced in between...and I remember what Ellie had said.

"John....she knew....Ellie was so sure that you will come back for me one day. She almost promised me that you would. She said that she had faith in our love."

"She was a good friend to me too", says John remembering.

It is true, I thought. Ellie always took his side even when he wasn't there.

"You know that she threatened me once?"

"Ellie threatened you John? Whatever for?"

"She said that she would hurt me badly if I ever broke your heart Cassie."

"..but Ellie would never hurt a soul! She was a non-violent person...she wouldn't even get angry at anyone,", I say surprised.

"She said that if I hurt you in any way, shape or form that she would get her lawyer parents to sue me. I was seventeen, I almost believed her. She was quite convincing!"

I laugh and say," That sounds so much like a Ellie thing to do!"

"Yes...I knew then that I would have to deal with being sued if I ever went on a date with you Cassie and it didn't go well. Luckily, it turned out alright", says John smiling.

I warm at the thought of Ellie looking out for me without me knowing.

"I miss her."

"I know you do Cassie. Try to think about her in her happier days. She would want you to be happy too."

John would comfort me during my grief and also helps me to forgive myself for Ellie's death. I fall in love with John again.

How could I not?

Maybe I was never out of love to begin with and had been waiting for him as well. In all the years since, no other person had come close to my heart and soul like John had.

If Ellie were alive today she would say, "I knew he would come back for you, all you needed was to believe in love Cassie. I am so happy....it is all so romantic!"

Chapter Forty-One: Adieu, My Dear Friend

L ife goes on after Ellie's death. The world didn't stop or slow down after she was gone...though to me it felt that it did. She had appeared suddenly in my life all those years ago and even more quickly she had gone from it. People tell me to move on, but how could I, without it feeling like a betrayal to Ellie?

Without realizing it, I have begun to fear living. My heart remained rooted to one spot, I didn't want to make new memories as I feared that I might forget what went before it.

I remember the tattoo that she had gotten, an infinity symbol wrapped around a heart made of thorns and roses. How ironic was the infinity symbol! The body that had gotten it inked was only mortal after all and now laid buried under the earth. She had said that life was made of both thorns and roses. I wished I had plucked away the thorns from her life, so that it would have simply left a row of roses for her.

I became a writer by profession and writing becomes my catharsis. I write and write my thoughts on paper, often holding back my grief as I don't get to share this experience with Ellie. I didn't get to be a writer while she had lived. I want to write about how she had been, to capture her nuances and immortalize it for the world. Ellie as her sweet, funny and loving self.

$$\infty\infty\infty$$

My only connection to her are my dreams and memories, when I dream about her, it is then that I see her most vividly. Ellie looks like her old self, healthy, happy and warm, a spectre of what she had been in life.

"You are going?", I say sadly.

She smiles. "You know that I am already gone."

"What if I need you?"

"Oh Cassie, my pineapple, you won't. Remember my braids? Remember how you opened my braids because you didn't like them being tied up. My time here is done, don't tie me to this world any longer Cassie."

I do remember and my own words echo in my mind from my distant past: "I want you to be free", says a young Cassie from my memory.

But I don't want her to go. My heart selfishly wants her to stay. "Please stay Ellie, don't leave me."

"Cassie...I need you to start living again."

"Living again? I am breathing aren't I?"

"Living is more than just breathing. Think about all the happy memories we shared together..."

"Happy? Ellie...how will I be even ok without you?"

"Cassie, my love, as long as you can think of one happy thought and smile, you will be ok. Life passes in the blink of an eye...it did for me. Cherish it while you are living, love yourself and those around you, open your heart and fear life no longer. Farewell, my friend. Farewell. Don't mourn my death, celebrate my life and yours. Our friendship made mine beautiful."

I wake up from my dream to find the sun shining golden and bright. She was gone. Ellie was gone.

I try to remember her words as she lived. "Love laughs eternal", I say sadly.

Chapter Forty-Two: Purgatory

I guess this is the part of the story where I should say, 'I smile at the memories and I live my life for love. I do it for her'...but this is not how it will go.

Why do Ellie's memories somehow seem more real to me than my present reality? The past is entrenched in my heart, soul and mind. It is entrenched in my every breath, it is there in every heart beat, it is entrenched in every fibre of my being.

I have a lot to be grateful for in my life but sometimes some things, some moments and some people leave such a mark on your life, that life begins to be defined by the moment before and the moment after their arrival.

I am stuck in that eternal prison and can't seem to get out of it.

On the anniversary of Ellie's death, many years later I decided to get the same tattoo as hers in her memory. The image of the heart of thorns and roses and the infinity symbol has haunted my dreams in the years since Ellie's death.

What it means to me I cannot say, I just know what it meant to Ellie. At least I can say that it will link me back to that happy moment when all was well.

I return back from the tattoo parlor, feeling the dull throbbing in my arm. I take an painkiller and get ready to fall asleep. I look at the tattoo as I drift off to sleep, wondering if it will still haunt my dreams tonight.

Silence and darkness. I do not have a single dream, nightmare or vision.

Perhaps finally I have been cured.

As I wake, I hear a familiar sound calling my name.

"Cassie! Cassie! Come see my tattoo!"

It's Ellie! My mind jolts and I wonder if I was too quick to think that my nightmares had gone away.

"....Ellie?"

"Yes Cassie...who else would it be?"

I rub my eyes to see Ellie still standing there beaming at me. She brings forward her arm for me to see the identical tattoo as the one I got peering at me.

I look to my arm and mine is still there. If this is not a dream, it feels too real.

"Ellie...you are alive?"

"Yes Cassie, I feel so alive!"

"No I mean that you are breathing.."

"I know right! I should have gotten this tattoo ages ago. I finally feel like I am in my skin and this is what was missing."

"But you were dead Ellie?"

Ellie looks at me puzzled. "Did you have a nightmare Cassie? You don't look so good. No worries, I am here and brought you some world famous croissants that will cheer you up and cure all."

She rushes to set up a table and I can't stop staring at her alive again. So what happened? I remember getting the tattoo and thinking that Ellie was dead...but nothing else seems as clear anymore...perhaps it was really a nightmare.

"Ellie I thought I lost you forever."

"Whoa there Cassie, have you been going through my movie scripts and rehearsing my lines? Leave the melodramatic parts to me ok."

I still don't understand what was going on, the only thing that confirmed what I knew to be true was the tattoo on my arm. Other than that, the life that I woke up to was the life that was in my past.

I try to explain this to Ellie.

"So you are trying to tell me that I died in the future and that you never got over the grief, despite finding John....and me haunting you in your dreams telling you incessantly and repeatedly to just let me go and move on?"

"Pretty much...yeah."

"That is a little crazy Cassie."

"But it is true, look at my tattoo!"

"I don't see anything Cassie.."

"It's right there, how can you not see it?!"

"Maybe you have not been eating enough and had a nightmare? You shouldn't worry Cassie. I am here, nothing happened to me."

"But you died of drug overdose. If the present now is real, I can't lose you again!"

"Cassie you know I never took drugs in my life, remember the campaign I started in High School? The one that said: 'I don't take candies from strangers'."

I start to remember and I believe that she was telling the truth. Perhaps life gave both of us a do-over. I could not bear the guilt of not being there for her during her drug addiction. Perhaps this Cassie was different from the one I knew.

∞∞∞

Things were the same in many way with Cassie but it some ways it wasn't. It was true that this Cassie didn't do drugs. I puzzled over the pieces from the past life and the current.

It was like there were different jigsaw puzzles but all of them completed the same final picture. I made some of the same old memories with Cassie, going over conversations that I had gone over before...but once in a while, I would make a new memory with her.

"Let us do a search for John!"

"What do you mean?"

"Let us search for him on social media. I can tip my fans and they can do the sleuthing for us! I have the best fans..."

Strange. This is not how I met John in -what I call now- my other reality. I look at her puzzled, which Ellie being Ellie, took as a sign of confirmation.

Her devoted fans managed to find John within a week and Ellie set us up with a meeting, the three of us. It is what I had dreamed when she had passed away before I had reunited with John in my other reality. Now we all got to be together again.

John meets us and we fall in love again. Ellie is ecstatic and already starts to dream up a wedding for the two of us. Years past and the moment finally arrives when the two of us decide to marry. Ellie is thrilled to be my maid -of-honor and wants to be the wedding planner too.

I see her as she prattles away at her dream wedding plan for John and I. It is so good to see her happy and in my life again. Many times I feel the other reality was just a mirage...that is until I see my arm amd the tattoo inked there permanently.

Ellie has settled on a destination wedding for us and I simply agree with whatever John and Ellie decide to do. Since she will be shooting for a pivotal scene for a movie around the same period, she will arrive on a flight earlier than us. She will take over the wedding arrangement before our wedding day and leave the next morning soon after the ceremony.

I sigh, relieved at my change in fate and as I do many times, glance over my forearm to see that this time the tattoo, along with the nightmares of the past, had also disappeared.

What I took to be a sign of good fortune, the disappearance of the tattoo, would however stand to mean something else entirely. Days before my wedding, as Ellie was set to arrive at our wedding destination before us, her plane crashed into the ocean.

187 passengers were onboard at that plane, including Ellie, and there were no survivors.

No. This can't be happening again.

My new life turned to a new nightmare. My life became dark, just like before, but this time with new regrets that I didn't have before or could have imagined. Ellie never got to be in our wedding in this life.

She reunited John and I, unlike in the other reality, where we were reunited after her death but cruelly she was gone again before we said our I dos.

Was I destined to this grief?

Years past again as I grieve her death and like before, the past starts to haunt my dream again.

What did it mean seeing those dreams again from a lifetime ago?

Final Chapter: Eternally Bound

T his time I dream about thorns and roses. I am in a forest clearing with a maze in the centre formed of rose bushes. I am lost and there is thick mist everywhere. I see an infinity symbol light up in the path ahead. As I reach for it, I hear a familiar voice again.

"Cassie! You would never guess who I found today!"

Just like before, I would rush to see if the voice was a vision but Ellie was really there, holding a small puppy in her arms, looking suspiciously like mini Buddy.

"It's a puppy! The sweetest creature I ever came across in my life. He just started to follow me on my walk and when I called him, 'Hey little buddy, what are you doing here?' he jumped into my arms!"

"You are here Ellie?"

"Yeah I forgot to call but isn't this pup so cute! He doesn't have a collar or is chipped...I will put up missing posters everywhere, just in case. But can we keep him if no one shows up?"

I nod, still too stunned to say anything.

"Yay! Can you hold him while I take a picture for the missing poster signs? Smile!"

In death or in life, or if I were given a choice to go to Heaven or Hell, I would go to where I could see Ellie again. For the memories and moments with her and everything that is good that comes with her friendship, I would choose to be eternally bound to her. And this is exactly what I chose.

I found that each time after Ellie's death in another lifetime, I would start to get the nightmares again. Following the heart of roses and thorns and the infinity symbol, I would be offered a choice to be with Ellie or to simply move on with my life without her. Every time I chose Ellie and I would wake to find her alive again, as if nothing had changed and we would go through life as best friends would.

In each reality, every time that her life is unexpectedly cut short, my pain is unbearable, and her death cleaves my heart in two again.

It seems that I held the golden thread of fate in my hand and it would be my choice to create another short life with Ellie or keep living with the grief to my own final days.

When John had said in my first life when I was sixteen, that I had an old soul, he was not right then but he would be right now. I have lived a thousand lifetimes. His words prophesized my destiny in a way he nor I could not have imagined.

It might seem like madness but I am happy with the memories that I get to make with Ellie in each lifetime. In each life, she is the one who links me back to John and Buddy and all that I love. My mind floods with memories of Ellie, of her during our childhood, of us as teenagers, of us struggling to be adults, of her in every moment since, both of us happy and laughing together.

I would continue this for an eternity or until when the fates decide to give up on our tragic destiny, finally letting us live our lives fully as it could be.

Our love and friendship will truly be eternal, my dear Ellie. I will never give up hope.

I had asked you in the beginning, what would you do for your best friend? This is what I have done.

I have tempted Fate and lived a thousand lifetimes just so Ellie gets the life that she deserves to have, one filled with happiness, not one brutally cut short from her loved ones. Hours after hours, days after days, weeks after weeks, months after months and years after years, I wandered this Earth to find peace with Ellie's Fate.

I had said that Ellie was my best friend and I would do anything for her, that means even becoming her emissary to the other world.

You might have heard of how Orpheus enters the underworld in order to bring his love Eurydice back to the world of living? or how Aeneas in Virgil's Aeneid seeked to enter the underworld and was asked by Priestess Cumaean Sibyl, who bridged the two worlds, to find the golden branch in order to do so? Aeneas was guided by birds to that Fated branch just like I was guided by the rose, thorn and infinity symbol to one of the Morais.

I hold on to the thread of Ellie's fate in my hands and refuse to let it go. I have held on to it for so long but things might finally change...

"I know what you are looking for", says the lady, even before I utter a single word. She has an ageless amd unremarkable face, all except for her bright silver eyes....and she also wore a crown made of roses. She is clothed in a white robe and carries a rod in her hand.

"What do you think I am here for?"

"Redemption...but not for yourself but someone close to you."

"How can you be so sure that is what I want?"

"My dear, you didn't say that I was wrong now did you?"

"It is true that I am not here for myself. I have questions about someone else, but you seem to know what I should be asking for?"

"I do but you might not like what I am about to tell you."

"I have tried every possible thing. I have had a thousand life-times to do it...but my soul is weary and I don't know how much longer I can hold on."

"Then let go my child."

"That I cannot do. I can't give up for Ellie's sake."

"I should have been clearer, you need to let go. Your friend has paid the price for her choices in her first life. The time has finally come. She will be reborn anew, as will you."

"I will be born anew?"

"Yes but at a price....you will not remember your past lives and you get this one chance."

"I won't remember....then how would I save Ellie at this one chance if I don't remember?"

"Your soul will know, it will remember at key moments the

lessons of the past...in the form of premonition, a gut instinct, a sense of foreboding....but in order for your friend to live the life that you desire, key elements will have to fall in place, over which you have no control. Your destiny and your friends' are weaved together but they are also other players that you don't know about."

"What do you mean? What key elements...what other players?"

"The best I can explain to you is as such: your friend's life has pieces not falling where they should, like missing puzzle pieces, and so her picture remains incomplete. You know it is true in the way her life was cut short in each lifetime. For her picture to be complete, three things are vital: she needs to feel her parent's affections, she needs her true love's reunion and she needs your unwavering support as her best friend."

"Her parents? They do love her, I saw their anguish at her death. True love's reunion? Ellie was never in love, was she?...and my unwavering support? She has that always!"

"Of the three missing elements, you can only do your part, give her unwavering support...but that would mean you will let go of the outcome. You can no longer linger, only then can the story unfold as it should."

"How will I know that her life is as it should be?"

"You will have to trust. Just as you have learned in your thousand lifetime, so will have the others. Trust in their love and yours. Trust in Ellie to make the right choices for herself."

"I will have to trust?"

"Yes, have faith for your friend."

"I will do anything for Ellie."

"My dear, you already have. It is up to your friend now. Just have faith in her."

"I believe in Ellie, she will make things right."

"I know, you are a dreamer my child. For your sake, your friend has been given this chance."

"Who are you? How do you know all this?"

"I am Lachesis of the three Moirai. It is me who measures the golden thread of fate that you hold in your hands and refuse to let go. I have come to complete my task."

How did it all come to this?

Ellie had kept secrets from me and everyone else. I am certain now that I dont' even know her full story. What secrets was she hiding from her best friend?

The most perplexing of them all: Who was her true love?

Made in the USA
Columbia, SC
22 June 2020